PENGUIN CLASSICS

The Judge's House

'I love reading Simenon . . . . . . think of Chekhov'
—William Faulkner

'A truly wonderful writer . . . marvellously readable – lucid, simple, absolutely in tune with the world he creates'
– Muriel Spark

'Few writers have ever conveyed with such a sure touch, the bleakness of human life'
– A. N. Wilson

'One of the greatest writers of the twentieth century . . . Simenon was unequalled at making us look inside, though the ability was masked by his brilliance at absorbing us obsessively in his stories'
– *Guardian*

'A novelist who entered his fictional world as if he were part of it'
– Peter Ackroyd

'The greatest of all, the most genuine novelist we have had in literature'
– André Gide

'Superb . . . The most addictive of writers . . . A unique teller of tales'
– *Observer*

'The mysteries of the human personality are revealed in all their disconcerting complexity'
– Anita Brookner

'A writer who, more than any other crime novelist, combined a high literary reputation with popular appeal'
– P. D. James

'A supreme writer . . . Unforgettable vividness'
– *Independent*

'Compelling, remorseless, brilliant'
– John Gray

'Extraordinary masterpieces of the twentieth century'
– John Banville

GEORGES SIMENON

The Judge's House

Translated by HOWARD CURTIS

PENGUIN BOOKS

PENGUIN CLASSICS

UK | USA | Canada | Ireland | Australia
India | New Zealand | South Africa

Penguin Books is part of the Penguin Random House group of companies
whose addresses can be found at global.penguinrandomhouse.com.

First published in French as *La Maison du juge* by Éditions Gallimard 1942
This translation first published 2015

011

Copyright 1942 by Georges Simenon Limited
Translation copyright © Howard Curtis, 2015
GEORGES SIMENON ® Simenon.tm
MAIGRET ® Georges Simenon Limited
All rights reserved

The moral rights of the author and translator have been asserted

Set in 12.5/15pt Dante MT Std
Typeset by Palimpsest Book Production Ltd, Falkirk, Stirlingshire
Printed and bound in Great Britain by Clays Ltd, Elcograf S.p.A.

ISBN: 978-0-241-18845-3

www.greenpenguin.co.uk

MIX
Paper from
responsible sources
FSC® C018179

Penguin Random House is committed to a
sustainable future for our business, our readers
and our planet. This book is made from Forest
Stewardship Council® certified paper.

Contents

Contents

The Judge's House

1. *The Customs Officer's Wife*

'Fifty-six, fifty-seven, fifty-eight . . .' Maigret counted.

He didn't want to count. It was mechanical. His head was empty, his eyelids heavy.

'Sixty-one, sixty-two . . .'

He glanced outside. The bottom halves of the windows in the Café Français were frosted. Above the frosted section, all you could see were the bare trees on the square and the rain, the never-ending rain.

'Eighty-three, eighty-four . . .'

He was standing there, his billiard cue in his hand, and he could see himself in the mirrors that covered the walls of the café.

And Monsieur Le Flem, the owner, carried on playing, never saying a word, quite relaxed, as if this was all perfectly natural. He would go from one side of the green baize to the other, bend down then straighten up again, watching the movement of the balls with a distant look in his eyes.

'A hundred and twenty-two . . . A hundred and twenty-three . . .'

The room was vast. Near the window, the maid, a middle-aged woman, was sewing. That was all. Nothing but the three of them! With a cat sitting by the stove.

And it was only three o'clock! And it was only 13 January.

Maigret could see the figure on a big calendar hanging behind the cash register. And it had been like this for three months! And . . .

He hadn't complained to anybody. Even Madame Maigret didn't know why he had fallen into disgrace and been transferred to Luçon. This was the hidden face of the profession, of no concern to those outside.

Madame Maigret was here, too, in an apartment they had rented above a piano shop, and they had already had some brushes with the landlord because . . . Well, never mind!

'How many points is that?' Monsieur Le Flem asked, not sure when to stop.

'A hundred and fifty . . .'

Maigret puffed gently at his pipe. Come on! A hundred and forty-seven, a hundred and forty-eight, a hundred and forty-nine, a hundred and fifty! The balls froze on the billiard table, the whites a nasty yellow, the red an unhealthy pink. The cues were placed back in their rack. Monsieur Le Flem went to the beer pump and poured two glasses, taking the heads off them with the help of a wooden knife.

'Cheers.'

What else could they have said to each other?

'It's still raining . . .'

Maigret put on his overcoat, placed his bowler hat well forward on his head and, a few moments later, his hands in his pockets, was walking along the streets of the town in the falling rain.

He opened the door to his office, its walls covered with administrative posters. His nose puckered at the smell of

Inspector Méjat's brilliantine, a sickly odour that even ten pipes could not have overcome.

An old lady in a bonnet, with a shrivelled face, was sitting there on a chair, holding a huge dripping umbrella, of the kind common in the Vendée, in front of her. There was already a long trail of water on the floor, as if a dog had been caught short.

'What is it?' Maigret asked, walking through the barrier and leaning down towards his one inspector.

'It's for you. She only wants to talk to you.'

'What do you mean, to me? Did she say my name?'

'She asked for Detective Chief Inspector Maigret.'

The old woman realized they were talking about her and pursed her lips in a dignified manner. Before taking his coat off, Maigret, out of habit, fiddled with some of the papers awaiting him on his desk: the usual routine, a few Poles to keep an eye on, missing identity cards, rescindments of residence permits . . .

'I'm listening, madame. Please stay where you are. But before we start, I have a question for you: who told you my name?'

'My husband, inspector . . . Justin Hulot . . . When you see him, you're bound to remember him, he has the kind of face you can't forget. He was a customs officer in Concarneau when you were there on a case. He read in the paper that you'd been appointed to Luçon . . . Yesterday, when he realized the body was still in the room, he told me . . .'

'Excuse me! What body is this we're talking about?'

'The one in the judge's house.'

Clearly a woman who wouldn't be easily intimidated! For the moment, Maigret was looking at her without a great deal of interest, not suspecting that this sixty-four-year-old woman he had before him, Adine Hulot, would soon become much more familiar to him and that, like everyone else, he would end up calling her Didine.

'First of all, I should tell you that my husband has retired and that we've moved to the village I come from, L'Aiguillon . . . I have a little house there, near the harbour, which I inherited from my late uncle . . . I don't suppose you know L'Aiguillon?

'That's what I thought. In that case, it won't be easy for you to understand . . . But who else could I turn to? Not the local policeman, who's drunk all day long and can't be bothered . . . The mayor's only interested in his mussels . . .'

'His mussels?' Maigret echoed.

'He's a mussel farmer, like my late uncle, like almost everybody in L'Aiguillon. He breeds mussels . . .'

That idiot Inspector Méjat saw fit to laugh sarcastically at this, and Maigret threw him an icy glance.

'You were saying, madame . . .'

She didn't need any encouragement. She was taking her time. She, too, had underlined with a glance the inappropriateness of Méjat's laughter.

'There are no stupid professions.'

'Of course not! Please go on.'

'The village of L'Aiguillon is quite far from the harbour. Not many people live there, only about twenty. The largest house is the judge's . . .'

'One moment. Who is this judge?'

'Forlacroix, his name is. He used to be a justice of the peace in Versailles. I think he got into trouble, and it wouldn't surprise me to hear that the government forced him to resign . . .'

She clearly didn't like the judge! And, small and wrinkled as she was, it was obvious this little old woman wasn't afraid to express her opinions about people!

'Tell me about the body. Is it the judge?'

'Unfortunately not! That kind of person never gets murdered!'

Excellent! Maigret had his answer, and Méjat laughed into his handkerchief.

'If you don't let me tell the story in my own way, you'll get me all mixed up . . . What day is it today? The 13th . . . My God, I hadn't even thought of that . . .'

She hastened to touch wood, then to make the sign of the cross.

'It was the day before yesterday, in other words, the 11th. The previous evening, they'd had people over . . .'

'Who's "they"?'

'The Forlacroixs . . . Dr Brénéol, with his wife and daughter, I mean his wife's daughter, because . . . It's a long story . . . Anyway, they'd had their little party, as they do every two weeks. They play cards until midnight, then they make a great racket starting their cars . . .'

'You seem to know a lot about what goes on in your neighbours' house.'

'I told you, our house – or rather, my late uncle's house – is more or less behind theirs. So even without meaning to . . .'

A gleam had come into the inspector's eyes that would have pleased Madame Maigret. He was smoking in a particular way, with short puffs, and he went and stoked the stove and then stood there with his back to the fire.

'About the body . . .'

'The next morning . . . I did say it was the 11th, didn't I? . . . The next morning, my husband took advantage of the fact that it was dry to prune the apple trees. I held the ladder. From up there, he could see over the wall. He was level with the first floor of the judge's house . . . One of the windows was open . . . Suddenly he comes back down and tells me, just like that:

'"Didine . . ." My name's Adine, but everybody calls me Didine . . . "Didine," he says, "there's someone lying on the floor in the bedroom . . ."

'"Lying on the floor?" I said. I didn't believe it. "Why would they be lying on the floor when there are plenty of beds in the house?"

'"That's the way it is . . . I'm going back up to have another look . . ."

'He goes back up. He comes down again . . . He's a man who never drinks and who, when he says something . . . And he's a man who thinks. After all, he was a public employee for thirty-five years . . .

'All day, I can see him thinking, thinking. After lunch he goes for his walk. He stops off at the Hôtel du Port . . .

'"It's odd!" he says when he comes back. "Nobody came in on the bus yesterday and nobody saw any cars."

'It was bothering him, you see? He asks me to hold the

ladder for him again. He tells me the man is still lying on the floor . . .

'That evening, he watched the lights until they went off . . .'

'What lights?'

'The lights in the judge's house. The thing is, they never close the shutters at the back. They think nobody can see them. Well, the judge came into the room and stayed there for a long time.

'My husband got dressed again and ran outside . . .'

'Why?'

'In case the judge got the idea of throwing the body in the water . . . But he came back soon after . . .

'"It's low tide," he says. "You'd have to wade through mud up to your neck . . ."'

'The next day . . .'

Maigret was dumbfounded. He had seen some strange things in the course of his career, but these two elderly people, the retired customs officer and Didine, spying on the judge's house from their home, keeping the ladder up . . .

'The next day, the body was still there, in the same position.'

She looked at Maigret as if proclaiming: 'You see, we were right!'

'My husband watched the house all day. At two o'clock, the judge went for his usual walk with his daughter . . .'

'Ah! The judge has a daughter . . .'

'I'll tell you about her some other time! A whole other kettle of fish, that one! He also has a son . . . But it's too

9

complicated to . . . When your man there behind us has stopped laughing, I may be able to continue . . .'

One in the eye for Méjat!

'Last night, high tide was at 9.26 in the evening . . . He still couldn't do anything, you see? . . . Up until midnight, there are always people around. After midnight, there wouldn't have been enough water any more. So my husband and I decided that, while he kept his eye on them, I'd come and see you. I took the nine o'clock bus. That gentleman told me you might not be coming today, but I realized he was trying to get rid of me. My husband said to me: "Tell the inspector that it's the customs officer from Concarneau, the one who has a little defect in his eye . . . And also tell him that I looked at the body through sailors' binoculars, and the man isn't someone from around here . . . There's a stain on the floor that must be blood . . ."'

'Excuse me,' Maigret interrupted. 'What time is the bus for L'Aiguillon?'

'It's already gone.'

'How many kilometres, Méjat?'

Méjat had a look on the wall map of the region.

'About thirty.'

'Phone for a taxi.'

He didn't care if Didine and her customs officer were crazy! He was prepared to pay the taxi fare out of his own pocket!

'If you don't mind stopping the cab just before the harbour, so that I can get out and they don't see me with you. It's better to act as if we don't know each other. People in

L'Aiguillon are so suspicious . . . You'll be able to stay at the Hôtel du Port. It's the better of the two. That's where you'll see just about everybody after dinner. If you can get the room that looks out on the roof of the ballroom, you'll even be able to see the judge's house . . .'

'Inform my wife, Méjat.'

Night had fallen, and the world seemed to have turned to water. The old woman appreciated the comfort of the taxi, which had previously been a chauffeur-driven car. The crystal flower holder delighted her, as did the electric ceiling light.

'I say, the things they make! The rich are so lucky.'

The marshes . . . Vast flat expanses, crisscrossed by canals, with the occasional low farmhouse, known as cabins in the Vendée, and the piles of cow pats which, when caked, are used as fuel . . .

Something was stirring dimly in Maigret's soul, a kind of hope. He didn't yet dare give in to it. Could it be that right here, deep in the Vendée, where he had been exiled, chance was going to bring him . . .

'I almost forgot. This evening, high tide is at 10.51 . . .'

Wasn't it staggering to hear this little old lady speaking with such precision?

'If he wants to get rid of the body, he'll take advantage of that. There's a bridge over the Lay that reaches to the harbour. From eleven o'clock, my husband will be on the bridge. If you want to talk to him . . .'

She knocked on the glass.

'Drop me here. I'll walk the rest of the way.'

And she plunged into the liquid darkness, her umbrella

swelling like a balloon. Soon afterwards, Maigret got out
of the taxi outside the Hôtel du Port.

'Want me to wait?'

'No, you might as well go back to Luçon.'

Men in blue, some of them fishermen, others mussel
farmers, and bottles of white and rosé wine on long tables
of varnished pitch pine. Then a kitchen. Then a ballroom
that was only used on Sundays. It all smelled new. White
walls. A ceiling of white pine. A staircase as flimsy as a toy
and a room that was also white, an iron bedstead covered
in gloss paint, cretonne curtains.

'Is that the judge's house I can see?' he asked the maid.

There was light at a dormer window which probably lit
the stairs. They tried to persuade him to use the dining
room, which was reserved for summer guests, but he preferred the main room. He was served oysters, mussels,
shrimp, fish and a leg of lamb, while the men talked among
themselves, in a strong accent, about things to do with the
sea, especially concerning mussels. Maigret understood
none of it.

'Have you had any visitors lately?'

'Not for a week . . . Or rather, the day before yesterday
. . . No, it was the day before that . . . Someone got off the
bus. He dropped in to tell us he'd be coming for dinner,
but we didn't see him again . . .'

Maigret kept bumping into things: rails, baskets, steel
ropes, crates, oyster shells. The whole seashore was
crammed with the sheds where the mussel farmers kept
their equipment. A kind of wooden village without

inhabitants. A wailing every two minutes: the foghorn from the Baleines headland on the Ile de Ré, so he had been told, on the other side of the straits.

There were also vague intermittent lights in the sky: the beams from two or three lighthouses disappearing into the mist.

The murmur of water in motion. The waves pushing back the current from the little river, swelling it, and soon – at 10.51, the old woman had said – the tide would be high. In spite of the rain, two lovers stood right up against one of the sheds, lips together, not speaking, not moving.

He looked for the bridge, an interminable wooden bridge, barely wide enough to let a car pass. He made out masts, boats bobbing on the waves. Turning, he could see the lights of the hotel he had just left, then two other lights, a hundred metres further on, those of the judge's house.

'Is that you, inspector?'

He gave a start. He had almost bumped into a man, whose eyes he now saw squinting at him from close quarters.

'Justin Hulot. My wife told me . . . I've already been here for an hour, in case he took it into his head to . . .'

The rain was cold. Icy air rose from the water of the harbour. Pulleys squeaked, invisible things lived their nocturnal lives.

'Let me bring you up to date. When I went up the ladder at three o'clock, the body was still there. At four o'clock, I decided I'd like to see it once again before nightfall . . . Well, it wasn't there any more. *He* must have taken it down. I suppose he's keeping it ready behind the door so as to save time when the moment comes . . . I wonder how he's going to carry it. The judge is shorter and thinner than me. About the same height and weight as my wife . . . The other man, though . . . Shhh! . . .'

Someone passed in the darkness. The planks of the bridge shook one after the other. When the danger was over, Hulot resumed:

'On the other side of the bridge is La Faute. Not even a hamlet. Mostly small villas for people who come here in the summer. You'll be able to see it when it's light . . . I found out something that may be of interest. On the night of the card game, Albert went to see his father . . . Careful! . . .'

It was the lovers this time, who had climbed on to the bridge and were now leaning on the parapet and watching the river flow by in the darkness. Maigret's feet were cold. Water had seeped into his shoes. He noticed that Hulot was wearing rubber boots.

'It's a 108 tide. At six in the morning, you'll see them all going to the mussel fields . . .'

He was speaking in a low voice, as if in church. It was at once unnerving and a little grotesque. From time to time, Maigret wondered if he wouldn't have been better off in Luçon, playing cards at the Café Français with the owner, Dr Jamet, Bourdeuille the ironmonger, and senile old Memimot, who always sat behind them and shook his head at every hand.

'My wife is watching the back of the house . . .'

So the old lady was still involved, was she?

'You never know. In case he might have got the car out and had the idea of taking the body further away . . .'

The body! The body! . . . Was there really a body in all this?

Three pipes . . . Four pipes . . . From time to time the door of the hotel opened and closed, and footsteps could be heard moving away, voices. Then the lights went out. A rowing boat passed beneath the bridge.

'That's old Bariteau on his way to laying his eel nets. He won't be back for another two hours.'

How could old Bariteau see his way in all this blackness? God knows. You sensed the presence of the sea, very close, just at the end of the narrows. You could breathe it in. It was swelling, irresistibly invading the straits.

Maigret's mind wandered, he couldn't have said why. He thought of the recent merger of the Police Judiciaire and the Sûreté Générale and of certain points of friction that . . . Luçon! He had been sent to Luçon, where . . .

'Look . . .'

Hulot gripped his arm nervously.

No, it really was unbelievable! The idea that these two old people . . . That ladder held by Didine . . . The naval binoculars . . . And those calculations of tides! . . .

'The lights have been switched off.'

What was so extraordinary, at this hour, about seeing all the lights go out in the judge's house?

'Come. We can't see well enough . . .'

All the same, Maigret found himself walking on tiptoe in order not to shake the planks of the bridge. That siren lowing like a hoarse cow . . .

The water had almost reached the wooden sheds. A foot struck a broken basket.

'Shhh!'

And then they saw the door of the judge's house open.

A short, sprightly man appeared in the doorway, looked left and right and went back into the passage. A moment later, the improbable happened. The little man reappeared, bent over, gripping a long object that he started dragging through the mud.

It must have been heavy. After four metres, he stopped to catch his breath. The front door of the house had been left open. The sea was still twenty or thirty metres away.

'Oof . . .'

They sensed that 'oof', sensed the physical effort he must be making. The rain was still falling. Hulot's hand trembled convulsively on Maigret's thick sleeve.

'You see!'

Oh, yes! It had happened just as the old woman had said, just as the former customs officer had predicted. That little man was clearly Judge Forlacroix. And what he was dragging in the mud was definitely the lifeless body of a man!

2. 'Hold on a Minute . . . '

What gave the scene a somewhat ghostly character was that the judge didn't know. He thought he was alone in the emptiness of the night. From time to time, the halo of the lighthouse brushed over him, and they were able to make out an old gabardine, a felt hat. Maigret even noticed that he had kept a cigarette between his lips, although the rain must have extinguished it by now.

There were now only four metres between them. Maigret and Hulot were standing near a kind of sentry box. They didn't even think of hiding. The only reason the judge didn't see them was quite simply because he didn't turn his head in their direction. He was having a lot of difficulty. The burden he was dragging had come up against a rope stretched across the embankment, some twenty centimetres above the ground, and had to be carried across. He went about it clumsily, obviously unused to manual labour. It was clear, too, that he was hot, because he wiped his forehead with his hand.

It was then that Maigret, without choosing his moment, without thinking exactly what he had to do, simply said:

'Hold on a minute . . .'

The judge turned his head and saw the two men: Maigret enormous, the customs officer tiny. It was too dark to make out any particular expression on his face. A few seconds went by, seeming quite long. Then a voice – a little shaky, perhaps? – was heard:

'I'm sorry! Who are you?'

'Detective Chief Inspector Maigret.'

He had stepped forwards, but still couldn't see much of the face. His feet almost touched the body, which seemed to be wrapped in sacks. At such a moment, why did the judge react by saying in a tone of surprise tinged with respect:

'Maigret from the Police Judiciaire?'

People were asleep in the surrounding houses. Old Bariteau, somewhere in the rustling darkness, was looking for holes in the seabed to place his eel nets.

'Maybe it's for the best.'

It was the judge speaking again.

'Would you like to come inside?'

He took a few steps, as if forgetting his package. There was such an oppressive calm around them that they had the impression they were living in slow motion.

'Perhaps it would be more convenient to take the body back indoors?' the judge suggested, reluctantly.

And he bent down. Maigret helped him. They did not close the door behind them. Hulot stood there in the doorway, and Forlacroix, who had not recognized him, was wondering if he was going to make his mind up to come in.

'Thanks a lot, Hulot!' Maigret said. 'I'll see you tomorrow morning. In the meantime, I'd prefer it if you didn't say anything. Do you have a telephone, Monsieur Forlacroix?'

'Yes, but we aren't connected after nine o'clock in the evening.'

'One moment, Hulot. Can you go and find someone at the post office? Ask to be put through to number 23, in Luçon. It's a hotel. Ask to speak to Inspector Méjat and tell him to come and join me as soon as possible.'

There! Now it was just the two of them, face to face in the passage, and the judge had switched on the light. He took off his hat, which was dripping with water, and his raincoat. The mysteries of the night had faded. What appeared in the light was a short, thin man with regular features, his face haloed by fine long blond and grey hair that looked like a wig.

He looked at his dirty hands, then at his burden. Maigret now noticed that the body had been wrapped in two coal sacks, one for the head and chest, the other for the legs. The two sacks had been clumsily tied together with string.

'Do you want to see him straight away?'

'Who is he?' Maigret asked.

'I have no idea. Take your coat off and come this way, please . . .'

He wiped his hands with his handkerchief, opened a door, switched on another light, and they found themselves on the threshold of a vast room, at the far end of which logs crackled in a fireplace.

At that moment, nothing could have been a greater surprise to Maigret than the pleasant warmth of this room, its brightness, its harmonious layout. Oak beams gave the impression that the ceiling was very low. They even had to descend two steps to enter. The floor was made up of white flagstones, over which two or three rugs had been thrown. And the white walls were lined with nothing but bookshelves, containing thousands of books.

'Please sit down, inspector . . . I seem to recall that you like heat . . .'

More books on an antique table. Two armchairs by the fire. Hard to believe that behind the door, sewn into two coal sacks . . .

'It's really lucky for me that I'm dealing with a man like you. I'm a little puzzled, though. I thought you were in Paris and . . .'

'I've been transferred to Luçon.'

'All the better for me. I'm sure it would have been hard to make myself understood by an ordinary police officer . . . Do you mind if I . . . ?'

From a Renaissance chest, he took a silver tray, a bottle and some crystal glasses, and these objects, artfully lit, glittered magnificently. There was an atmosphere of refinement and comfort about it all . . .

'Please have a glass of armagnac. By the way – it's only just occurred to me – how did that ugly, one-eyed old customs officer come to be involved in . . .'

It was only now, at this precise moment, that Maigret became fully aware of the situation. He literally saw himself, sitting comfortably in his armchair, his legs stretched towards the fire, warming his glass of armagnac in the hollow of his hand. He realized that it wasn't he who was talking, asking questions, but this short, thin, calm man, the same man who, only a few minutes earlier, had been dragging a dead body to the sea.

'Forgive me, Monsieur Forlacroix, but perhaps I could take the opportunity to ask you a few questions.'

The judge turned to him with a mixture of surprise and reproach, his eyes blue as forget-me-nots. He seemed to be saying:

'Why? I thought you were a different kind of person . . . Well, as you wish . . .'

But he said nothing. He bent his head slightly, politely, the better to listen. It was a gesture he made often, and which indicated that he was a little hard of hearing.

'You told me earlier that you don't know that . . . that man . . .'

My God, how hard it was! How difficult the simplest things became when you had let yourself sink into such a state of bliss!

'I don't know him from Adam, I assure you.'

'In that case, why . . .'

Come on! It had to be done! Maigret all but closed his eyes, as if swallowing a bitter pill.

'Why did you kill him?'

He looked. And saw again the same surprised, reproving expression on the judge's face.

'But I didn't kill him, inspector! Come now! Why would I have killed someone I don't know, someone I never saw alive? I know it may be difficult to accept, but I'm sure a man like you will believe me.'

The most remarkable thing was that Maigret already

believed him! It was as if he were under a spell in this silent house where nothing could be heard but the crackling of the logs and where, during the silences, you were aware of the distant murmur of the sea.

'If you so wish, I'll tell you exactly what happened. A little more armagnac? An old friend of mine, who used to be public prosecutor in Versailles, sends it to me from his chateau in the Gers.'

'You lived in Versailles too, didn't you?'

'Almost my whole life. A charming town. The people there still seem to be living in the court of Louis XIV, and I think it would be difficult to find elsewhere a society that was more polite in the old sense of the term. We formed a little group that . . .'

A gesture of the hand, as if to chase away pointless memories.

'That's of little importance . . . It was . . . Let's see now, it was Tuesday . . .'

'Tuesday the 10th,' Maigret said. 'You had friends over, if I'm not mistaken . . .'

The judge smiled slightly. 'I see you're well informed. You were with Hulot earlier. It wouldn't surprise me if you'd seen Didine. She knows what happens in my house better than I do . . .'

A thought suddenly struck Maigret. He looked around, sensing that something was missing in this house.

'Don't you have a maid?' he said, surprised.

'Not a live-in one. An old woman and her daughter who live here in L'Aiguillon come every morning and leave again immediately after dinner . . . Anyway, on

Tuesday, my friends came as they do every two weeks. Dr Brénéol, who lives one kilometre from here, his wife and Françoise . . .'

'Françoise is Madame Brénéol's daughter?'

'That's correct. From her first marriage. That's of no importance, except for Brénéol . . .'

And a slight smile hovered again over his lips.

'The Marsacs, who live in Saint-Michel-en-l'Hermitage, arrived a little later . . . We played bridge.'

'Was your daughter with you?'

A moment's hesitation. A touch more gravity in his gaze.

'No, she was in bed.'

'And tonight?'

'She's in bed . . .'

'Didn't she hear anything?'

'No. I took care to make as little noise as possible . . . Anyway, on Tuesday, we finished about midnight.'

'And you had another visitor,' Maigret said, turning towards the fireplace. 'Your son.'

'Albert, yes. He only stayed a few minutes.'

'Doesn't your son live with you?'

'He lives near the town hall. We don't exactly have the same tastes. My son is a mussel farmer . . . As I'm sure you've already been told, that's the main activity around here.'

'Would it be indiscreet of me to ask why your son paid you a visit in the middle of the night?'

The judge stared at his glass, was silent for a moment, then finally said:

'Yes!'

And he waited.

'Did your son go upstairs?'

'That's where he was when I saw him . . .'

'I assume he went to say hello to his sister?'

'No. He didn't see her.'

'How do you know?

'Because, I might as well tell you straight away, given that you'll hear it from other people, I'm in the habit of locking my daughter in her room at night . . . Let's just say she's a sleepwalker . . .'

'Why did your son go upstairs?'

'To wait for me, because I had friends downstairs. He was sitting on the top step. We had a short conversation . . .'

'On the stairs?

The judge nodded. Weren't they starting to get into the realms of the implausible? Maigret swallowed the contents of his glass in one go, and Forlacroix refilled it.

'I went downstairs to put the chain on the door. Then I went to bed, read a few pages and fell asleep almost immediately. The following morning, I went to the fruitery to get . . . To be honest, I find it hard to remember what I went there for. It's a room we call the fruitery because it's where we keep the fruit, but there's actually a bit of everything there. A junk room, if you prefer . . . There was a man lying dead on the floor, a man I'd never seen before. His skull had been smashed in with what you people call a blunt instrument. I searched in his pockets . . . In a while, I'll show you the objects I found there . . . But no wallet. Not a single paper that could identify him.'

'What I don't understand . . .' Maigret began.

'I know! That's going to be the hardest thing to explain! I didn't call the police. I kept the body in the house for three days. I was waiting for the tide to be favourable so that I could get rid of it at night, in secret, like a murderer . . . And yet, I'm telling you the honest truth, I didn't kill the man. I had no reason to do so. I have absolutely no idea why he was in my house. I don't know if he broke in while he was alive or if someone brought him here when he was already dead.'

Silence fell. Again the distant moan of the foghorn could be heard. There were boats out at sea. Fishermen were lifting nets heaving with fish up on deck. Had Hulot managed to make his phone call? If he had, the unbearable Méjat, with his brilliantined hair, must be getting hastily dressed right now. Did he have yet another conquest in his bed, as he liked to boast?

'Well,' Maigret sighed, drowsy from the heat, 'I don't think this is going to be an easy matter!'

'That's what I'm afraid of, too. Given the situation, I mean since the man was dead, it would have been preferable . . .'

He didn't finish his sentence, but looked towards the windows. The ebb tide would have carried him away, and nobody would have been any the wiser! Maigret started to move, shifted one leg, then the other, until at last he was able to get out of the excessively deep armchair; it looked as if his head might touch the beams.

'Shall we go and have a look at him anyway?'

He couldn't help admiring this low room, where it

was so pleasant to spend time, where everything was so precisely in its place. He looked up at the ceiling: who was this girl who was locked up for the night?

'We could take him into the laundry,' the judge suggested. 'It's at the end of the passage.'

Now they were both trying to avoid getting themselves dirty. They were no longer out in the wet night. They had become civilized men again.

The laundry was vast, covered in red tiles. There was still linen drying on iron wires.

'Do you have a pair of scissors?' Maigret grunted, touching the two sacks. Coal-black water oozed out.

The judge couldn't find any scissors but came back with a kitchen knife. The fire was out. It was cold. Their wet fingers were turning red.

The most extraordinary thing about all this was that it wasn't tragic. The judge showed no horror at the prospect of seeing again the face of the man he had sewn into the sacks. Maigret was wearing his stubbornest, grouchiest expression, but the truth was that he was basking almost voluptuously in this investigation that had fallen into his lap, right here in Luçon, where he had been exiled. He was like a seal that had been juggling in circuses and now found itself back in the icy seas of the North!

How long had it been since he had last entered a house, as he had done earlier, and sniffed about, come and gone, heavily, patiently, until the souls of both people and things no longer held any secrets for him?

And that Didine with her Hulot! And that son waiting for his father, at midnight, sitting on the stairs!

Now for the other man! The victim! What would emerge from these filthy sacks?

For a moment, it was almost comical. You expect all kinds of things, but what real life throws up is always more bizarre. So it was that now, when the upper sack was removed, the face they uncovered was completely black. Because of the coal, of course!

It was only natural, but for a moment the two men looked at each other, and both had the same idea; for a split second, they had the absurd impression that they were in the presence of a negro.

'Do you have a towel and a little water?'

The tap made a racket. When the noise ceased, Maigret listened out. Another noise could be heard outside, that of a car engine. A door slammed. A bell rang loudly in the passage. Méjat didn't do things quietly!

'Where's the detective chief inspector?'

He saw him standing there. Méjat had a red nose and a lock of hair hanging askew.

'Did I get here fast enough? Shall I keep the taxi, chief? Is there really a body? Where's the crazy old lady?'

He had brought with him, on his person and in the folds of his clothes, some of the cold damp air from outside and also a crudity that altered the quality of the atmosphere. Now it was less muted, less muffled. Méjat, with his strong Toulouse accent, wasn't sensitive to nuances.

'Have you identified him, chief?'

'Not at all!'

Maigret was surprised at his own words, words that belonged to the past, words he had often repeated in the old days when he was floundering in a complicated case, and fools like Méjat . . .

'He received quite a blow to the head!'

The judge looked at Maigret, Maigret looked at him, and both were thinking the same thing, regretting the almost intimate peace of a little earlier. As for Méjat, he was looking through the dead man's pockets and, of course, finding nothing.

'How old do you think he is, chief? I'd say about forty . . . Are there any labels on his clothes? . . . Do you want me to strip him?'

'Go ahead! Strip him!'

Maigret filled a pipe and started to walk up and down the laundry, talking to himself in a low voice.

'I'll have to phone the public prosecutor in La Roche-sur-Yon . . . I wonder what he'll decide.'

And the judge, standing there in front of him, uttered gravely, not realizing how comical he sounded:

'It would be a *disaster* if they put me in prison.'

'Come now, Judge Forlacroix,' Maigret burst out, unable to stop himself. 'Don't you think it's a *disaster* for this man to have lost his life and to be lying here on these tiles? Don't you think it's a *disaster* for a wife, children perhaps, to be wondering what's become of him? And that it would have been even more of a *disaster* never to find out, because someone else preferred not to complicate his life?'

He wasn't even grateful! He had been given a wonderful armagnac, a log fire as penetrating as balm, an hour of gentle bliss, and here he was turning against his host, becoming once again the implacable Maigret of Quai des Orfèvres.

The mild Monsieur Forlacroix's only response was a reproachful look.

'There's a label in the jacket!' Méjat cried triumphantly. 'Let's see now . . . Pa . . . Pa . . . Pana . . .'

'Panama!' Maigret grunted, snatching the garment from his hands. 'That's going to make things easier for us, isn't it? A man who wears clothes made in the Republic of Panama! Why not China?'

The uppers of the shoes had to be cut in order to take them off. It was again Méjat who saw to this, and this young man who dressed so sharply, and was so happy to play the ladykiller, performed his task as naturally as he would have written a report, with the names circled, as he was in the habit of doing.

'The shoes are from Paris, Boulevard des Capucines. The heels are already a bit scuffed. In my opinion, they've been worn for at least a month. What do you think he could have been, chief? A Frenchman? . . . I think he was a Frenchman. A fairly well-to-do sort, who didn't work with his hands . . . Look at his hands.'

Neither of them gave a thought to the taxi waiting outside, or to the driver pacing up and down to warm himself. Abruptly, the door flew open. A man appeared at the end of the passage, as tall and broad as Maigret, wearing thigh-length rubber boots. On his head he had a sailor's sou'wester. His upper body was encased in an oilskin jacket beneath which he was obviously wearing a few thick sweaters.

He advanced, heavy and suspicious. He looked first Maigret, then Méjat up and down, bent over the body and finally stared at the judge.

'What's going on?' he snapped, almost threateningly.

Forlacroix turned to Maigret.

'My son . . .' he said. 'I'd be grateful if you'd explain to him . . .'

And with that, he quickly left the laundry with little mouse-like steps and went back to the low room where he had first received the inspector.

'What's going on?' the young man repeated, this time addressing Maigret. 'Who is this? Who killed him? You're police, aren't you? When I saw a car outside the house . . .'

It was already five o'clock in the morning! Albert Forlacroix had been on his way to the mussel fields when he had spotted the taxi.

'The driver told me he'd brought an inspector from Luçon.'

And suddenly, with a frown:

'My sister . . . What has he done to my sister?'

He was so anxious that Maigret had a kind of shock. Could it be that . . . While he and Forlacroix had sat there in soft armchairs, in front of the crackling logs . . .

'I'd like to see your sister, as it happens,' he said in a changed voice. 'Do you have a key to her room?'

The other man merely shrugged his massive shoulders.

'Méjat . . . Wait down here.'

Their steps made a noise on the stairs, then in the long corridor, which turned several corners.

'It's here . . . Could you stand back?'

And Albert Forlacroix lunged at the door.

3. The Airaud Trail

It was an extraordinary moment, and Maigret would never forget the taste of it. First the late-night weariness, and that smell of wet wool. That unknown corridor that seemed to go on for ever. Again they heard the foghorn. Just as Albert Forlacroix launched himself at the door, Maigret looked towards the stairs and saw the judge, who had walked up without making a noise. Behind him, still in the stairwell, Méjat's face . . .

The door yielded, and his impetus carried Albert right into the middle of the room.

It was unexpected. It was like nothing that might have been foreseen.

The room was lit by a bedside lamp with a finely gathered pink silk shade. A young girl lay on a Louis XVI bed. She was in an almost seated position, because she had lifted herself on one elbow, and, in the movement she had made to look towards the door, a swollen, heavy breast had escaped from her nightdress.

Maigret could not have said if she was beautiful. Was the face too broad perhaps, the forehead too low, the nose childish? But her lips were as full as a ripe fruit, and her eyes were huge.

Had she switched the lamp on when she had heard

noises in the corridor? Had she been asleep? It was impossible to know. She didn't seem very surprised. And yet she could see the great bulk of Maigret in the doorway and her brother standing in his rubber boots in the middle of the room.

All she did was murmur in a calm voice:

'What's the matter, Albert?

Her father had not come in, but he had approached the door and had heard. Maigret was embarrassed, unable to take his eyes off that breast, and Albert had noticed. Not that he paid any attention. He looked suspiciously about the room then went and opened a door.

Was it intuition? Maigret felt sure this door led to the famous fruitery, and he stepped forwards.

'What are you looking for?' he asked.

No reply, just a nasty look. Then suddenly Albert Forlacroix bent down. On the floor, both in the bedroom and in the fruitery, there were footprints. A man's shoes had left thin rings of mud, and the mud wasn't completely dry.

'Who is it?'

Albert walked to the window of the fruitery. It was half-open, letting cold air filter in.

Maigret returned to the bedroom to find the girl in the same position, her breast still bare. So there had been a man in this room, in this bed, during the night, perhaps when Maigret was already in the house . . .

Albert strode across the room. Maigret followed him. The judge, waiting in the corridor, murmured:

'I won't be able to lock the door again . . .'

His son shrugged and, ignoring everyone, started down the stairs, with Maigret at his heels.

'Méjat!'

'Yes, chief . . .'

'Keep an eye on the house . . . From the outside.'

He took his coat off the hook and grabbed his hat. It wasn't light yet, but the harbour was bustling, and voices and various noises could be heard from all sides.

'You didn't answer me just now. Do you know who the man is?'

Pretending not to see Hulot, who had been waiting for him, Maigret walked right past him, leaving the former customs officer quite crestfallen.

As for Albert, he was in no hurry to speak. A strange young man!

'Can I go and harvest my mussels? Or do you intend to arrest me?'

'You can harvest your mussels. Unless you have something to tell me. Like the name of the man whose prints you found in your sister's room.'

Suddenly Albert stopped and put his hand on Maigret's shoulder. They had reached the edge of the water. The land fell away rapidly, uncovering an expanse of brownish, swollen mud. Men, women in trousers, all of them in rubber boots, were loading empty baskets into flat boats that were then pushed out with the help of poles.

'The man? Let's see . . . It's him over there . . .'

A young man almost as tall and strong as Albert, dressed

just like him, was helping an old woman into his boat and then immediately cast off from the shore.

'His name's Airaud . . . Marcel Airaud.'

With that, Albert opened the door of one of the sheds and came out again with a pile of baskets.

The maid at the Hôtel du Port was already up and was washing down the tiled floor when Maigret returned.

'Where have you been?' she said, surprised. 'Didn't you sleep in your bed?'

He sat down by the stove and asked for coffee, bread, sausage and cheese. Only then, comfortably wedged into his wall seat, did he ask as he chewed:

'Do you know a man named Airaud?'

'Marcel?' she replied, so quickly that Maigret looked at her with rather more attention.

'Marcel Airaud, yes.'

'He's a local lad. Why do you ask me about him?'

It would have been difficult for her to pretend that this particular young man was of no interest to her.

'Is he a mussel farmer? Married?'

'Not at all!'

'Is he engaged?'

'Why do you ask me that?'

'No reason. I got the impression he's been hanging around the judge's daughter . . .'

'First of all, it's not true!' she cried through clenched teeth. 'Others, maybe! And they don't need to hang around, or stand on ceremony, because if you really want to know, that girl's a . . . a . . .'

She looked for the worst swear word she could find, but

in the end it was quite an innocuous expression that fell from her lips:

'. . . a good-for-nothing! Everybody knows that. If her brother had had to keep beating up the men who visit her in her room . . .'

'Are there many of them?'

'Almost all! And the time she ran away to Poitiers, where they found her in a real state! . . . If anyone's been trying to convince you that she and Marcel . . .'

'Could I have a little more coffee, please? One more question: the man who came by bus on Tuesday . . . What time did he arrive?'

'It was the four-thirty bus.'

'Did he leave straight away?'

'He said he'd be back for dinner. He set off in the direction of the bridge, I think. It was already dark.'

'Would you recognize him if you were shown his photograph?'

'Maybe . . .'

'All right! I'm going to bed.'

She looked at him in astonishment.

'Let's see, now. It's six o'clock. Wake me up at eight, with some very strong coffee. Can I rely on you, young lady? You're not angry at me because of Marcel?'

'Why should I care about that?'

He slept soundly. It was a great gift of his, being able to sleep anywhere, at any time, and forget his worries from one second to the next.

And when the maid, whose name was Thérèse, woke

him with piping-hot coffee, a pleasant surprise awaited him. Everything had changed. Sunlight was coming in through the window. The hubbub of life filled the room, a commotion made up of a thousand noises from all sides.

'Would you be so kind as to bring me up some soap, my dear? If they sell safety razors locally, buy me one, and a shaving brush.'

As he waited, he leaned out of the window and drank in the cold air, as delicious as spring water. So this was the harbour that had seemed so dark and clammy last night? That was the judge's house? And the sheds on the shore . . .

Everything gave him a delighted sense of astonishment. The sheds, for example, were brightly painted, in white, blue and green. The judge's house was all white, covered in delicate pink tiles.

It was a very old house, which must have undergone a lot of changes over the centuries. It was a surprise, for example, to discover, next to the window of the fruitery, quite a vast terrace surrounded by a balustrade with an enormous green porcelain pot at each corner.

Below, beyond the garden, another house, also white, no upper floor, probably just two rooms, with a little garden and a fence, a ladder propped against an apple tree. Wasn't that Didine, in her white bonnet, standing in the doorway, her hands on her belly, looking in Maigret's direction?

The mussel farmers were already coming back. Twenty boats, thirty boats, strange flat craft called acons, had moored at the dock, and baskets and baskets of blueish mussels were being hoisted into big lorries with spluttering engines.

'I could only find a cheap throwaway razor for three francs fifty, but the shopkeeper says . . .'

The throwaway razor would have to do! Maigret wasn't sleepy any more. He was as fresh as if he had spent all night in his bed. A little glass of white wine downstairs before he went out? Why not?

'Would you like me to polish your shoes?'

Of course! No more mud! Everything clean! He couldn't help smiling when he spotted Inspector Méjat in the distance, looking like a wet cockerel drying its feathers in the sun.

'Nothing new, my friend?'

'Nothing, chief. Two women arrived, an old one and a young one. The maids, I assume . . . Look.'

The three ground-floor windows were open. They were the windows of the library, where Maigret and the judge had spent part of the night by the fire. An old woman in a white bonnet was shaking the rugs, and a fine golden dust rose into the sun.

'What about the judge?'

'No sign of him. Or the girl . . . Oh, God, there's that oddball who's been bending my ear all morning.'

Maigret looked in the direction indicated and saw Hulot, squinting even more in the sunlight than at night. He was hoping they would call him over. He was only waiting for the signal and he would come running.

'Stay here until I get back. I won't be long.'

'Do I have time to get a cup of coffee?'

Permission granted! Maigret was in a good mood at this

stage. Soon afterwards, he walked into the police station and introduced himself to the sergeant.

'First of all, I need to use your telephone. Could you call the prosecutor's office in La Roche-sur-Yon for me?'

The prosecutor hadn't arrived yet. His deputy listened to the verbal report and approved it. Then Luçon. Then two or three more phone calls.

Yes, Maigret would manage to get things moving eventually. Of course, he felt nostalgic. In Paris, he would have had his whole team around him, fellows who knew his methods, to whom he would barely need to speak: Lucas, who had been promoted, Janvier, Torrence, the men in Criminal Records . . .

Here, he had to wait until midday for the photographer to arrive, and the gendarme on guard near the judge's house was looking at the passers-by so fiercely that they were starting to suspect something at the café on the corner.

Maigret rang the bell. The old woman opened the door.

'I'll go and see if Monsieur can . . .'

'Let him in, Élisa.'

He was standing in the library, where perfect order reigned, and the sun came in through the three windows.

'I've come to photograph the body. You left it in the laundry, I hope?'

'I'll give you the key. I locked it, to stop the maids from . . .'

'Do they know?'

'Not yet. I preferred . . .'

'Is your daughter up?'

What a question! Couldn't Maigret hear her playing the piano on the first floor?

'I assume she doesn't know either?'

'She knows absolutely nothing . . .'

Maigret had perhaps never before encountered such unflappability.

Here was a man with refined manners, a quiet, cultivated man who, at the end of a bridge party, finds his giant of a son sitting on the stairs and regards it as quite natural!

The following morning, he opens a door and discovers the body of a murdered man, a man he doesn't know.

He takes even that in his stride, doesn't mention it to anybody and goes for his usual walk with his daughter.

He waits for a favourable tide. He sews the corpse into some sacks. He . . .

The police are in his home. His son appears, in an excitable mood. The door to his daughter's room is broken down. It's clear that a man has spent part of the night there.

He remains calm. The maids arrive as usual, and the house is cleaned without any fuss. The young girl with the naked breast plays the piano. The father merely locks the door of the laundry where the corpse is . . .

The photographer got down to work, and the judge watched him as if it were the most natural thing in the world to sit a dead man up and try to give him the appearance of life.

'I must inform you,' Maigret grunted, 'that the prosecutor

will be here at about three in the afternoon. Until then, I don't want you to leave the house. The same goes for Mademoiselle Forlacroix . . .'

Why did it feel strange to say 'Mademoiselle Forlacroix'? Because he had seen her in her bed, one breast outside her nightdress? Because a man had left muddy footprints in her room?

'May I ask you if my son has spoken to you, inspector? You will have a glass of port, won't you?'

'Thank you. Your son simply pointed out a young man named Marcel Airaud. Do you know him?'

The judge blinked, and his nostrils became a little pinched.

'You also think it was this Marcel who was in your daughter's . . .'

A very low voice, a mere breath. 'I don't know . . .'

The door to the library was open. Logs were burning.

'Come in a moment, would you?'

It was a plea. He left the photographer at the door.

'I assume you've realized?'

Maigret said neither yes nor no. It was an embarrassing situation, especially dealing with a father.

'It's because of her that I left Versailles and moved here . . . This house has belonged to my family for a long time, and we'd sometimes spend a month here in the summer . . .'

'How old was she?'

'Sixteen. The doctors warned me that the episodes would be more and more frequent . . . At other times, she's completely normal . . .'

He turned his head away. Then, shrugging his shoulders:

'I didn't tell you about it straight away. I'm not too sure what I was hoping . . . You do understand now why it would have been better if the sea had carried the body away? They'll say . . . God knows what people's imagination will dream up! Not to mention that fool Albert . . .'

'What was he doing here that night?'

Too late. Already the judge's dismay had faded. For a few seconds, it had been possible to believe that he was melting, that he was going to open up.

Was it because Maigret had asked too specific a question? He looked at the inspector with his cold eyes, the pupils almost colourless in the sunlight.

'No, it wasn't about that! . . . It doesn't matter . . . Are you sure you wouldn't like some port? . . . I have a Portuguese friend who . . .'

One friend sent him armagnac, another port. Didn't he seem preoccupied with giving his life all the refinement he possibly could?

Through the gap in the curtains, he suddenly noticed the gendarme pacing up and down outside and gave a nervous little laugh.

'Is he here for me?'

'You know I have no choice . . .'

The judge sighed and said something unexpected: 'This is all very regrettable, inspector!'

Overhead, the piano was still being played, and Chopin's chords harmonized perfectly with the atmosphere of this grand house where life should have been so sweet.

'See you later!' Maigret said abruptly, like a man resisting temptation.

The men who had returned from the mussel fields were filling the main room of the Hôtel du Port. Who had spoken? Whoever it might have been, everyone watched Maigret as he sat down at a table with Méjat and ordered lunch.

Their blue clothes had been washed clean by the rain and the seawater into sumptuous shades. Thérèse, the little maid, was in an emotional state and, following the direction of her gaze, Maigret recognized Marcel Airaud, sitting among a group of men, drinking rosé wine.

A sturdy young man of about twenty-five, as heavy as the rest of them, especially in their boots, with a calm gaze and slow gestures.

The conversations, which had been noisy earlier, had ceased. The men turned towards Maigret. Then they took a slug of their drinks, wiped their mouths, looked for something to say, anything, just to break the embarrassing silence.

One of the older men left, then another.

'Off for my grub! The wife must be starting to belly-ache . . .'

Marcel was one of the last to remain, one elbow on the table, a cheek resting on his open hand. Thérèse came and asked Maigret:

'Would you like the mouclade?'

'What's that?'

'Mussels in cream. A local dish.'

'I can't stand cream,' Méjat declared.

When she walked away, Marcel stood up to take her place. He pulled over a straw-bottomed chair, sat down astride it and touched the brim of his cap.

'Can I talk to you for a minute, detective chief inspector?'

No humility. No bravado either. He was at ease.

'How do you know I'm a detective chief inspector?'

Marcel shrugged. 'People talk. Since we got back from the mussel fields, they've been talking . . .'

There were only two men left, both fishermen, listening from a corner. A clatter of plates came from the kitchen.

'Is it true that a man was murdered in the judge's house?'

Beneath the table, Méjat's knee touched Maigret's. The inspector, his mouth full, raised his head and looked calmly at Marcel, who did not lower his eyes.

'Yes, it is.'

'In the fruitery?'

This time there was a touch of dew-like moisture on his upper lip.

'You know the fruitery?'

Marcel didn't reply, but threw a glance at Thérèse, who was just then bringing the steaming mouclade. 'What day did it happen?'

'I'd like to ask you a question first. What time did you get home last night? You live with your mother, don't you?'

'Did Albert say something?'

'I'm asking the question.'

'It was just after midnight . . .'

'Do you usually leave the judge's house so early?'

44

Another glance, this time towards the kitchen, into which Thérèse had just disappeared.

'It depends . . .'

A pity this was happening just as the mouclade had arrived, because it was a masterpiece. In spite of himself, Maigret was trying to identify a taste of . . . what could it be? . . . a slight hint . . . barely an aroma . . .

'What about Tuesday?' he asked.

'I didn't go there on Tuesday . . .'

Maigret frowned, sat motionless for a moment, staring into space, then suddenly cried triumphantly:

'Curry! I'd bet anything you like there's curry in this . . .'

'Don't you believe me?'

'About Tuesday? I have no idea, my friend. How could I possibly know that yet? . . .'

'I'm ready to swear . . .'

Of course it would have been nice to believe him!

Just as it would have been nice to believe the judge! Just as you instinctively believed Albert!

All the same, the corpse hadn't got there by itself!

4. *Under the Eyes of* La République

All in all, Maigret had no cause for complaint. It all went well, very well even, and at the end Monsieur Bourdeille-Jaminet deigned to utter a few feeble words which must have been meant as congratulations.

It was Maigret who had chosen the town hall, because the police station was really too dark and smelled of old leather, cabbage soup and unwashed brats. The town hall had a spacious reception room, with dazzling whitewashed walls. There was a flag in a corner, a bust of *La République* on the mantelpiece and a pile of family record books on the green baize table.

The gentlemen arrived in two cars: first the prosecutor, Monsieur Bourdeille-Jaminet, so tall that his gaze seemed not to reach the ground, with his deputy, then an examining magistrate whose name Maigret did not catch, a clerk, the pathologist and a lieutenant of gendarmes.

Other gendarmes had arrived from Luçon and seen fit to set up what amounted to a roadblock in the street, which meant that people would have gathered even if they hadn't known anything was happening.

The body was already there, in the courtyard. The pathologist had asked permission to work in the open air. The trestle tables used for banquets had been brought out. Dr Brénéol had finally arrived, looking quite nervous. He was distantly related to the prosecutor. They exchanged polite remarks and talked about the will of some cousin by marriage.

Everyone was smoking. Beyond the glass door was the ballroom, still hung with paper chains from the most recent dance, the benches lined up against the walls for the mothers.

'Excuse me, gentlemen . . . My dear colleague, may I ask you to . . .'

The doctors in the courtyard. The legal people in the reception room, the clerk sitting behind a pile of papers. As for the mayor, he was waiting in the doorway with a self-important air, chatting with a police sergeant.

After a while, Maigret began wondering if anyone would talk about the case at all, so remote did everyone seem from the drama. The judge was telling a story about a duck hunt he had attended the previous winter on the headland near L'Aiguillon.

'Shall we both begin?' Maigret said to the clerk.

He dictated in a low voice, a very low voice in order not to upset the others. Had they learned anything new since morning? Nothing really, apart from the fact that Thérèse had identified the traveller who had got off the bus on Tuesday. The bus driver had also identified him immediately, but couldn't remember if the man had got on at Luçon or Triaize.

Photographs had gone out in all directions. All the gendarmes would be provided with them. They would be shown to innkeepers and hoteliers. The following morning's newspapers would publish the photograph. In other words, the usual routine.

'You're going to wrap this up nicely, aren't you, inspector?' the magistrate asked pleasantly, as if awarding Maigret a good mark.

The doctors returned, unfazed, and washed their hands at the drinking fountain behind the mayor's office . . . A blunt instrument, as expected . . . The blow had been a violent one . . . The cranium had been shattered . . . The stomach contents would be examined later . . .

A strong, healthy fellow . . . The liver a little enlarged . . . He must have liked his food . . .

'I'm sure, my dear prosecutor, that my friend Forlacroix, with whom I played bridge that night, had nothing to do with this . . .'

'Shall we go, gentlemen?'

In a procession, on foot, because it wasn't worth getting in the cars. With the populace following on! And that cheerful sun up above . . .

'After you, prosecutor . . .'

The door opened without their having to ring the bell. Old Élisa showed everybody in. Judge Forlacroix was standing self-effacingly in a corner of the library. It was embarrassing: they wondered if they should say hello to him, shake his hand . . .

'I put keys in all the doors, gentlemen . . .'

His daughter, Lise, sat in an armchair, watching them with large astonished eyes, and a ray of the setting sun set a lock of red hair ablaze. Well, well! The night before, Maigret hadn't noticed that she was a flaming redhead.

'If you'd like to show us the way, inspector,' the prosecutor sighed, a man of the world apologizing for intruding in someone else's house and anxious to get it over with as quickly as possible.

'This way . . . This is the girl's room. The judge's room is at the end of the corridor . . . The fruitery is here . . .'

Six men in coats and hats, looking around them, bending down, touching the odd object, nodding.

'There are tools in this cupboard. There's a hammer here that the killer could have used, but I haven't found any prints . . .'

'Gloves, do you think?' the prosecutor uttered from his great height, as if saying something very intelligent.

It was a little like a tour of a house where the contents were being auctioned off. Were they going to visit the judge's room? Maigret opened the door. The room was of average size, furnished soberly but with taste. That same mixture of almost peasant simplicity and refinement.

Inspector Méjat was outside. Maigret had entrusted him with the task of keeping an eye on the onlookers, observing the reactions of certain people, listening in on conversations. Didine was in the front row, shaking her head, outraged at being left with the crowd, since it was she, after all, who'd done everything.

The magistrate and the prosecutor talked in low voices in a corner. The prosecutor nodded. He walked up to Maigret.

'I'm told you want him to be left free provisionally, at least for two or three days? . . . It's delicate, isn't it, very delicate, because the one thing we've established is that he was in possession of the corpse . . . Well, if you're prepared to take the responsibility . . . Your reputation . . .

We'll leave you an arrest warrant. Perhaps a blank warrant, too, what do you think? . . .'

Satisfied, he screwed up his eyes, which was his way of smiling.

'Well, gentlemen . . .'

They were leaving. It was over. Dr Brénéol apologized and said he would be staying in the house with his friend Forlacroix. It only remained for the others to get back in their cars. Raised hats. Handshakes.

A big sigh from Maigret.

Phew! Now he could begin his investigation!

There she stood before him, all thin, lips pursed.

'If you'd like to come and see me, I may have some things to tell you . . .'

'Of course, Madame Didine! Let's see, now . . . I'll drop by no later than this evening . . .'

She walked away, pulling her shawl tight across her chest. Groups were standing here and there. Everyone was watching Maigret. Children followed him, one of them imitating his heavy gait.

A little world was closing in on itself again. Now that the formalities were over and the magistrates had left, the village was going to resume its life, the only difference being that Maigret was now embedded in it, so to speak. Pointless to chase the kids away! They'd get used to him!

He saw the mayor standing in his doorway and went to say hello to him.

'It occurred to me, inspector . . . Obviously you'll need

a place to work . . . If you'd like me to give you the key to the town hall . . .

An excellent idea! That big white room was pleasant, and Maigret went there immediately, as if to accustom himself to the atmosphere and make himself at home. The stove on the right. He would have to light it every morning and keep stoking it. A place for his pipe and his tobacco. Beyond the window, a courtyard with a lime tree in the middle, then railings, and the street leading to the sea.

Who was that walking so quickly? Oh! It was only Méjat. He came in, out of breath.

'I think I have something new, chief . . . Marcel Airaud . . .'

'Well?'

'Something I heard, listening to people talking. Apparently when he left you earlier, he went straight to his boat . . . He has a motor-boat . . . People saw it moving off towards the end of the bay, over by Pont du Brault. There's no reason for him to go to that side. It isn't time to harvest the mussels.'

There was a telephone on the table. Maigret tried it.

'Hello, mademoiselle . . . Is there a telephone at Pont du Brault? . . . You say there's only one house . . . An inn? . . . Could you put me through? . . . Yes, Detective Chief Inspector Maigret . . . I'm at the town hall and I'll be disturbing you quite often . . .'

He looked at the electric lamp, which only gave out a yellowish light.

'Find me a forty candle-power bulb, Méjat . . . Hello? The inn at Pont du Brault? . . . I'd like to ask you for some

information, madame . . . No, this isn't the brewery . . .
Have you seen a little motor-boat this afternoon? . . . Yes,
from L'Aiguillon . . . You say he's moored outside your
place? . . . A bicycle? . . . Hello, are you still there? . . .
He had a glass of wine? . . . You don't know where he
went? . . . Towards Marans? . . . Thank you, madame . . .
Yes . . . If he comes back . . . Call the town hall of L'Aiguillon
immediately . . .'

He ran to the door. In the gathering dark, he had just
spotted the lieutenant of gendarmes getting ready to go
back to Luçon.

'Lieutenant! Will you come in for a moment? . . . I
assume you know Pont du Brault? What's it like?'

'It's all the way over there in the marshes. A canal
leads from the end of the bay to Marans, ten kilometres
inland. You're lucky to come across a cabin every three
kilometres.'

'Will you have your men search the region? I need to
find a man named Marcel Airaud, a tall fellow, one metre
eighty, a solid fisherman type, who's not exactly incon-
spicuous. He sailed from here in his boat and left it moored
near the inn at Brault. He took a bicycle . . .'

'And you think . . .'

'It's too soon to think anything, lieutenant. Can I count
on you?'

Would he go to see Didine before or after dinner? He
went before. Night had fallen. Pulleys were starting to
creak again, and the beams from two lighthouses crossed.

A twisted vine ran along the wall. The door and shutters
were painted green.

'Come in, inspector. I was wondering if I'd done any-thing to you . . .'

The cat jumped off a wicker armchair. Hulot stood up from his corner and respectfully removed a long meer-schaum pipe from his mouth.

'Please sit down, inspector. You will have a drink, won't you? Justin! Get the glasses from the cupboard.'

She wiped them. There was an oilcloth on the table and a very tall bed in a corner, covered in a huge red eider-down.

'Give the inspector the armchair . . . No, I insist! With all that's been happening, I let my fire go out. You can keep your hat on.'

She was talking for the sake of talking, but it was obvi-ous she was thinking about something and knew perfectly well where she was aiming. She didn't resume her seat. She didn't know what to do with her hands, which were constantly moving. And, since Maigret was doing nothing to help her, she had no choice but to ask, out of the blue:

'Did you find the child?'

What did she mean? Was there a child in this case?

'I didn't think anybody would mention him to you. People around here don't talk much, especially not to strangers. In a while, maybe, when they're used to you . . .

'But as I said to Hulot, I'm on your side.

'I saw you questioning Thérèse . . .'

How had she seen that? Was she spying on Maigret through the curtains? She was quite capable of that! She and her husband must be keeping track of the inspector and staying posted about everything he did.

'Old people like us, who have nothing to do, have time to think, you understand? Another glass? . . . I insist! It never did anybody any harm . . . Not you, Justin. You know perfectly well you can't take it.'

And she moved the bottle away from her husband.

'How old do you think Thérèse is? From the look of her, you'd think she's just a kid, but she must be about twenty-three. Even twenty-four wouldn't surprise me. Well, ever since the age of sixteen, she's been running after Marcel. Yes, I saw him talking to you as well! Built like he is, and with property, two houses that belong to him, and the mussel fields and everything, he has no trouble finding girls. Thérèse is quite common. In the summer, her mother sells mussels and oysters door to door around the villas on the other side of the estuary.

'All the same, she landed him! Everyone noticed, three years ago, how big she was getting.

'But these people have their pride. She left, supposedly to work in the city. When she came back a few months later, I swear she'd lost weight!

'And I know where she goes every month, when she has her two days off. She goes to Luçon, where she put her child in the care of a level-crossing keeper.

'What do you think of that?'

To be honest, he didn't think anything of it yet. Thérèse and Marcel . . . So Thérèse had a hold over him . . .

'I'm talking about three years ago, mind you! Since then Marcel has started spending his nights in the judge's house. I suppose you already know that. There have been others before him . . . Maybe even after him . . . Only, I'm going to tell you what I think. With him, it wasn't the same. The others took advantage of her. Men are like that . . .'

A sly little look at her husband, who squinted even more and assumed an innocent air.

'I'm sure Marcel was in love with her, and I bet that, if he'd been able, he would have married her, in spite of the fact that she's not like other girls . . .

'Now suppose Thérèse brought someone she knew from Luçon, a man capable of avenging her. It's easy enough to get into the judge's house. Look out here. It's dark, but you can see the white of the terrace. Any man could climb up there. From there, you can get over the stone rim and into the fruitery. The window's almost always half open. He may lock his daughter in, but it's as if I was trying to keep water in my hand.'

Maigret gave a start on becoming aware, suddenly, of the course of his own thoughts. For a few moments now, as he listened to the old woman's voice droning on, hadn't he started indulging in some absurd images, images that were still vague, of course, but which, if he wasn't careful, might take on shape and form?

' . . . It's easy enough to get into the judge's house . . .'

He again saw old Didine in his office in Luçon, he heard her clear voice, the almost staggering precision with which she had described the drama even though she hadn't even seen it!

Her faultless reasoning . . . Her meticulous calculation of the tides . . . Work a professional policeman would have been proud of . . . And the two of them keeping an eye on the house, one watching the back, the other the front . . . Even down to the naval binoculars! . . .

All the same, it was incredible. These ideas had to be dismissed; you only had to look at this room, a poor peasant room, with its bed, its eiderdown, the thick glasses on the oilcloth, Didine's white bonnet . . .

'So you didn't know the judge when he moved here?'

Something clicked. He was sure of it. A barely perceptible shock, a quivering of the muscles just under the skin.

'It depends what you mean by that. I knew him when I was very small. I was born in the house opposite the town hall. The judge used to spend his holidays here with his cousin. When his cousin died, he inherited the house.'

'Did he keep coming here after he was married?'

'Not every year!' she replied, suddenly laconic.

'Did you meet his wife?'

'I saw her, like everybody. A fine-looking woman!'

'Unless I'm mistaken, you're about the same age as Forlacroix, aren't you?'

'I must be a year younger than him.'

'You went to live in Concarneau with your husband, and he settled in Versailles. When you came back to L'Aiguillon, he was in the house and was already a widower.'

'He isn't a widower,' she said.

This made Maigret sit up in his wicker armchair, which creaked as he did so.

'His wife left him, but he isn't a widower.'

'Are you sure?'

'I'm sure he wasn't a widower a month ago, because I saw her with my own eyes, as clear as I'm seeing you now.

She got out of a car and knocked at his door. They stood there for a while in the passage, and then she left.'

He half expected her to tell him the registration number of the car. That would have been too good!

'It's your fault if you didn't know all this before. Instead of running around all over the place without coming to see me and without saying a word to my husband. I can admit this now. He was quite discouraged. Isn't that so, Justin? You can tell the inspector. He knows what it is to speak his mind, and that it's those who have nothing to be ashamed of who are never at a loss for words . . . Have your drink, inspector. What else would you like to know? It isn't that I've finished. The things I could tell you, we'd be here until tomorrow. But I have to wait for them to come back to me . . .'

It was enough! Too much, even! This little old woman was as calculating as a devil!

'It's like the doctor. I don't know if this is of any interest to you, but he's the judge's best friend. Have you seen his wife? A tall woman, a brunette, always heavily made-up, always with extravagant clothes. She has a daughter from her first marriage. You'll see her. Not much to look at. And yet Dr Brénéol is crazy about her and is constantly driving her around without his wife. They go as far away as possible. Even so, someone from here, whose name I could tell you, saw them coming out of a hotel in La Rochelle.'

Maigret was on his feet now, as exhausted as if he had been for a long walk.

'I'm sure I'll be back. Thank you.'

She must have thought there was now a conspiratorial

closeness between them, because she held out her hand and signalled to her husband to do the same.

'Don't hesitate to come again. And above all, you can be sure I'm telling you nothing but the truth . . .'

There was a lighted window in the judge's house, the window of Lise's room. Was she already in bed? He walked around the outside of the house. By now, the maids had left. Just the two of them within those walls . . .

He entered the already familiar main room of the Hôtel du Port and was struck by the glance that Thérèse threw him. She was clearly anxious! Wasn't she trying to see from his face if there had been any new developments?

Méjat was leaning on the counter, having an aperitif with the hotelier.

'Tell me, Thérèse, did you know that Marcel had to go to Marans?'

'Marans?' she repeated like someone on her guard, anxious not to betray herself.

'Since you're so close, I thought he might have told you . . .'

'He has no reason to tell me what he's doing . . .'

'What's for dinner?'

'Soup, plaice and, if you like, a pork chop with cabbage . . .'

'Let's eat, Méjat!'

The inspector had news for him. The victim, whose photograph had been shown to all the hoteliers in Luçon, hadn't slept in that town. They would have to wait. Especially for the newspapers . . .

'Aren't you tired, chief?'

'I'm going to bed as soon as I've eaten and I don't plan to get up before eight o'clock tomorrow morning.'

He was hungry. He managed to clear his mind of too many thoughts as he watched Thérèse come and go. She was fairly nondescript, and not in especially good health. The kind of little hotel maid you don't usually notice, with her black dress, her black stockings, her white apron. The place was empty. The men were at home, having their dinner, and wouldn't come back and spend an hour here until after they'd finished.

The telephone rang. It was under the stairs. Thérèse answered.

'Hello? . . . Yes . . . What do you . . .'

'Is it for me?' Maigret asked.

She listened.

'Yes . . . Yes . . . I don't know . . . Nobody mentioned it . . .'

'What is it?' the hotelier asked, from the kitchen.

Thérèse hurriedly put the receiver down. 'Nothing . . . It was for me . . .'

Maigret was already on the phone.

'Hello? . . . Detective Chief Inspector Maigret, mademoiselle . . . Can you tell me where the call you just put through was from? . . . What? . . . Marans? . . . Ask for the exact number, yes . . . Call me back . . .'

He went back to his table. Thérèse, looking quite pale, served him without saying a word. After a while, the phone rang again.

'From a café? . . . The Café Arthur? . . . Put me through to the police station in Marans, mademoiselle . . . Hello? . . . Are you the sergeant? . . . Detective Chief Inspector

Maigret . . . Go straight to the Café Arthur . . . Do you know it? . . . That's good . . . A man has just made a phone call from there . . . Someone named Marcel Airaud . . . Take him to the station and inform me immediately . . .'

A heavy silence. The pork chops. The cabbage. Thérèse coming and going without looking Maigret in the face.

Half an hour passed. The phone.

'Hello? . . . Yes? . . . Ah! . . . No . . . Wait for instructions . . . That's right . . .'

A pause. Thérèse still didn't dare turn towards Maigret, whose big back could be seen under the stairs. The inspector made a move with his hand, as if hanging up, but continued talking:

'He's wounded? . . . Take him to the prison in Luçon anyway . . . Thank you . . . Goodnight, sergeant . . .'

He returned heavily to his seat, sighed, wondered if he should have some cheese, winked at Méjat, then, taking advantage of the fact that Thérèse was in the kitchen, whispered:

'The rascal vanished immediately after his phone call . . . I wonder what he could have said to her . . .'

5. Someone Wants to Go to Prison

Was it really cruel? Thérèse hated him, of course. Every now and again, she would throw him such a black look that Maigret was forced to smile, and then she no longer knew what to do: rush at him and scratch his face or smile in her turn.

For more than an hour, he kept her dangling like a fish at the end of a line. Whatever she did – go in and out of the kitchen, try to eat at a corner of the table, respond when customers called her – she couldn't escape Maigret's tranquil gaze.

Perhaps, when it came down to it, that gaze attracted her? Wasn't this big, placid man, smoking his pipe and staring into space, more of a friend than an enemy?

She kept going from one extreme to the other, from excessive nervousness to anger to a degree of kindness. Having cleared the table, she came and asked:

'What will you have?'

But, after serving the calvados, she was obliged to rush into the corridor. When she came back, her eyes were red, and she was blowing her nose.

Men were playing cards, and she broke a glass as she served them. In the kitchen, she got up from the table without having eaten a thing.

Finally, she spoke to the hotelier's wife. From a distance,

you couldn't hear the voices, but you could guess from the way they held themselves. Thérèse looked as if she was ill and kept glancing up at the ceiling. The hotelier's wife shrugged.

'Go on, my girl!'

Thérèse took off her apron and came to see if anything remained to be cleared, throwing Maigret an insistent look as she did so.

'Before you go to bed, Méjat, make sure there's one gendarme keeping guard in front of the judge's house and one behind ... Another watching young Forlacroix's house ...'

He stood up and climbed the stairs, touching both the banisters and the wall. This whole part of the building was new. The wood was too bright, the walls rough, and you ended up with white on your clothes.

Maigret went into his room and left his door open. After a few minutes, he gave a start of surprise, became almost irritated, then glanced into the corridor and smiled.

The others below would still be there for an hour or two. Too bad if Méjat got ideas, hearing the chief inspector's voice in the maid's room! He went in. She was standing there, waiting for him. She had loosened the bun on the back of her neck and the dark mass of hair now framing her face made her features thinner and her nose more pointed, but also made her gaze less candid.

Sitting on the edge of the iron bedstead, Maigret examined her at his leisure, and it was she who had to speak first. 'I can tell you you're wrong to hound Marcel ... I know him better than anyone ...'

She was searching for the right tone, like an actor, but couldn't find it.

'The proof of that is that we were supposed to be getting married this summer . . .'

'Because of the child?'

She didn't show any surprise. 'Because of the child and everything. Because we love each other. Is that so strange?'

'What's strange is that the child is now three years old, and you're only now thinking of making it official . . . Look at me, Thérèse. I can assure you there's no point in lying. What did Marcel ask you on the phone?'

She looked at him for a long time, then heaved a sigh. 'Too bad if I'm making a big mistake . . . He wanted to know if they'd found a paper in his pockets . . .'

'Whose pockets?'

'The dead man's, I suppose!'

'And that's the question you answered no to?'

'I think if they'd found something important I'd have heard about it . . . Just because Marcel asked me that doesn't mean he killed . . . As I said before, we were supposed to be getting married . . .'

'And yet he's been seeing Lise Forlacroix in her room almost every night . . .'

'He's never loved her!'

'An unusual way not to love someone!'

'You know how men are. It isn't love, it's something else. He's often talked about it. It's a kind of vice, and he swore to me he'll get over it . . .'

'That's not true!'

With a sudden shudder, she turned hard and vulgar.

'What gives you the right to say it isn't true? Were you there? Is it also not true that I saw him coming out of the judge's house, not through the window, but by the front door? And that the judge was being nice to him? And that he knew about everything . . . Who's the decent one in all this? . . . I had a child, that's true. But I don't lure men to my room . . .'

'Hold on a moment! When was it that you saw Marcel with the judge?'

'Maybe a month ago . . . Wait . . . It was just before Christmas.'

'And you say they looked as if they were getting along? What did Marcel say when you asked him to explain?'

She was going to lie again. It could be seen from the way her nose quivered.

'He told me not to worry. That everything was fine. That in four or five months we'd be married and that we'd get a house on the other side of the straits, over towards Charron, so that we never have to see these people again . . . He loves me, do you hear? He had no reason to kill a man he didn't even know . . .'

Steps on the stairs, in the corridor. A door. It was Méjat coming back and whistling as he undressed.

'Is that all you have to tell me, Thérèse? Think carefully. Half of what you've told me so far has been the truth and half has been lies. Because of the lies, it'll be hard for me to take the truths into account . . .'

He had stood up. He was too tall and too broad for the room. Suddenly, just when he was least expecting it,

Thérèse threw herself on his chest and began sobbing desperately.

'There, there . . .' he said, as if calming a child. 'It's all right. Tell me what's on your mind . . .'

She sobbed so loudly that Méjat, who was opposite, opened his door.

'Calm down, my dear. You're going to wake the whole house. Don't you want to talk about it now? . . .'

She shook her head, still hiding her face in Maigret's chest.

'I think you're wrong. But there it is! Go to bed. Would you like me to give you something to help you sleep?'

Still like a child, she nodded. He put a sleeping pill in the tooth mug and ran some water.

'It'll be better tomorrow morning . . .'

She drank, her eyes and cheeks wet, and as she did so he backed out of the room.

He heaved a sigh of relief as he at last got into his bed, which, like Thérèse's room, was too small for him.

The following morning was sunny and very cold. Thérèse, as she served him his breakfast, looked more stubborn than ever. Méjat had got hold of some brilliantine from the barber's in L'Aiguillon and stank of it.

Maigret, his hands in his pockets, went for his little walk, watching the mussel farmers returning, the baskets of mussels, the greenish-blue sea in the distance, the bridge he had never been all the way across and beyond which were the beginnings of a seaside resort, a few holiday villas for people of modest means nestling among the pines.

A gendarme was stamping his feet in front of the judge's house. The shutters were open. All this constituted a delightful little world which was starting to become familiar to him. Some people said hello to him, others watched him suspiciously. He ran into the mayor, who was loading mussels on to a lorry.

'There are already some telegrams for you. I put them on your table in the town hall . . . I think the lieutenant is waiting for you . . .'

It was late. Maigret had slept in. Now he was calmly on his way to his office, just as in the old days, during slack periods, he would walk to Quai des Orfèvres through the Saint-Antoine district and across the Ile Saint-Louis.

The plaster bust of *La République* was in its place. The stove was purring. It must have been the mayor who had had the tactful idea of placing a sealed bottle of white wine and some glasses on the desk.

The lieutenant had come in with Maigret. The latter took off his hat and coat, and was about to ask a question when he was pleasantly surprised by a veritable explosion of children's cries. Right there, beneath his windows, in the sun, the whole school was having its break. Children went sliding across the frozen puddles, each time with a dull thud of clogs. There were red and blue and green scarves, pea jackets, shawls.

'Well, lieutenant, any news of Marcel Airaud?'

'No sign of him yet. The marshes are enormous. The cabins have to be searched one by one. At this time of year, some paths are barely passable. There are isolated cabins that can only be reached by boat.'

'And the judge?'

'All quiet. Nobody's been in or out of the house, except for the two maids this morning.'

'What about Albert Forlacroix?'

'He went out to the mussel fields as usual this morning. One of my men has his eye on him. Especially as they say he's a violent lad who loses his temper over nothing.'

Was it an affectation of his to warm himself with his back to the stove and slowly light his pipe when there were telegrams waiting for him on the table? Or was it rather a concern not to confuse things, to do everything in its own time, to have done with L'Aiguillon first before finding out what had happened elsewhere?

The first telegram, as if ironically, was from Madame Maigret.

Have put suitcase with linen and change of clothes on bus. Await news. Love.

'What time does the coach arrive?'

'A few minutes from now.'

'Would you be so kind as to collect a suitcase in my name and have it taken to the Hôtel du Port . . .'

Another telegram, a longer one, from Nantes.

Flying Squad Nantes to Detective Chief Inspector Maigret.

Stranger discovered L'Aiguillon identified. Stop. Dr Janin, 35, living Rue des Églises, Nantes. Stop. Left home

Tuesday 10 January without luggage. Stop. Inquiries continuing. Stop. Phone for further details.

The lieutenant had just returned. Maigret handed him the telegram and casually remarked:

'He looked older than he was.'

Then he turned the crank of the telephone, bade the postmistress a pleasant good morning and asked her to get him the flying squad in Nantes.

This was all good old traditional work. Let's see now! A third telegram, from Versailles, in response to a telegram from Maigret.

According to latest information, Madame Forlacroix, née Valentine Constantinesco, lives Villa des Roches-Grises, Rue Commandant-Marchand, Nice.

'Hello? . . . The flying squad in Nantes? Maigret . . . Put me through to him . . . Guillaume? That's right, old chap . . . Yes, fine . . . You've been quick . . . I'm listening, yes . . .'

Maigret never took notes. If he had a propelling pencil in his hand and a paper in front of him, it was only to make doodles that had no connection with the case.

' . . . Émile Janin . . . Faculty of Medicine in Montpellier . . . Very humble family from the Roussillon . . . One interesting detail: two years as an intern at Sainte-Anne . . . So, he's good at psychiatry . . . Ah-ha! . . . Quite independent-minded . . . Enlists as a naval doctor . . . What ship? . . . The *Vengeur* . . . The *Vengeur* went around the world three or four years earlier . . . That explains the clothes bought in Panama . . . Still too independent . . . Not a very good record . . . Returns to civilian life . . . Settles in Nantes where he specializes in psychoanalysis . . .

'Hello, mademoiselle? . . . One more call, if you don't mind . . . Could you put me through as a matter of priority to the Sûreté in Nice, Alpes-Maritimes? . . . I'm most grateful . . . Yes, I know you're doing what you can and, before leaving, I'll bring you some chocolates . . . You prefer marrons glacés? . . . Duly noted . . .'

And, addressing the lieutenant:

'I wonder if I'm not going to have to use my blank warrant . . .'

Was it intuition? He hadn't finished when the phone rang insistently. The children had gone back to class. It wasn't Nice yet, of course.

'Detective Chief Inspector Maigret? . . . One moment . . . Chief Prosecutor Bourdeille-Jaminet on the line . . .'

The voice was still distant, as if detached from material things:

'I gather he's been identified? . . . In these circumstances, I wonder . . . I've taken on a great responsibility . . . Do you still have your arrest warrant? . . . Well, inspector, in agreement with the examining magistrate, I think it would be prudent to . . .'

Méjat had come in and sat down quietly in a corner, from where he squinted at the friendly bottle of white wine.

'Nice!'

'Thank you . . . Sûreté Nationale? . . .'

He gave his instructions, in just a few words, and when he had finished he looked mechanically at the paper lying on his desk and saw that what he had drawn was nothing other than a full mouth, the kind of well-defined, sensual lips you see in the paintings of Renoir.

He tore the sheet of paper into little pieces and threw them in the fire.

'I think . . .' he began.

Someone was crossing the courtyard: old Élisa's daughter, who worked with her mother in the judge's house.

'Show her in, Méjat.'

'It's a letter for Monsieur Maigret.'

He took it, dismissed the girl and slowly tore open the envelope.

It was the first time he had seen the judge's handwriting, handwriting that was neat, small and careful, elegant but perhaps too refined. Not one line higher than the other. A paper that was plain, but of rare quality and in an unusual format.

Detective Chief Inspector,

Forgive me for writing you this note instead of visiting you in your office at the town hall or in your hotel. But, as I am sure you will realize, it is painful for me to leave my daughter unattended.

I have thought a great deal since our last conversation and have come to the conclusion that I need to make certain declarations.

I am perfectly willing to come and see you wherever and whenever you wish. I admit, however, even though this request may not be very proper, that I would prefer it if you could do me the honour of another visit.

Needless to say, I am at home all day, and whatever time you choose I will make mine.

Thanking you in advance for whatever you decide to do, inspector.

Respectfully yours.

Maigret stuffed the letter into his pocket without showing it to the lieutenant or to Méjat, both of whom were finding it hard to conceal their curiosity.

'How long ago were the newspapers delivered?' he asked.

'We should have copies any minute now. The bus that brings them in with the post arrived while you were on the phone.'

'Could you go and get me one, Méjat? And can you check once again that the judge didn't have any visitors this morning apart from his maids?'

He was less cheerful than he had been earlier. His gaze was becoming heavier. He kept moving objects around for no reason as he paced up and down the room. Then he stared at the telephone and finally turned the crank.

'It's me again, mademoiselle . . . I'll have to double the quantity of marrons glacés . . . Have you finished sorting the mail? . . . They haven't started delivering it yet? . . . No letter for Judge Forlacroix? . . . Tell me . . . Has he made or received any phone calls? . . . No? . . . No telegram either? . . . Thank you . . . Yes, I'm still waiting for an urgent call from Nice . . .'

71

Méjat returned, accompanied by three people, whom he left in the courtyard. As he came in, he announced:

'Reporters.'

'I see!'

'One from Luçon and two from Nantes. Here are the regional papers.'

Although they all published the photograph of the corpse, none of them, obviously, announced yet that the dead man had been identified.

'What shall I tell them?'

'Nothing.'

'They're going to be furious. You'll see them at lunch, they're all staying at the Hôtel du Port.'

Maigret shrugged and put some coal in the stove, then looked at the time, because he could already see the children coming out of school. What did they care, those people in Nice, in that sun that was like a metal disc?

One little detail was nagging at him, one point he couldn't clarify. Why had the judge written him this letter just when the body had been identified? Did he know? And if he did, how had he found out?

The telephone . . . Still not Nice . . . Marans informing him that there was still no trace of Marcel Airaud and that the search was continuing throughout the marshes . . .

Good! Nice, at the same moment . . . Three voices on the line . . .

'Hang up, Marans . . . Hang up, for heaven's sake . . . Hello, Nice? . . . Yes, Maigret . . . You say this person hasn't left Nice in the last three weeks? . . . You're sure of that? . . . No telegram yesterday or this morning? . . . What? . . . I didn't quite catch the name . . . Luchet . . . Van Uchet? . . . Could you spell it? . . . V for Victor . . . Van Usschen . . . Yes, I'm listening . . . A Dutchman . . . Cocoa . . . Yes, send me everything you can! . . . If I'm not here, leave a message with my inspector . . .'

He said in a low voice, more to himself than to the others:

'The judge's wife has been living for several years in Nice with a man named Horace Van Usschen, a wealthy Dutchman who made his fortune in cocoa . . .'

Then he opened the bottle of white wine and drank a glass, two glasses, looking at Méjat as if not seeing him.

'Don't move from here until I get back.'

The three reporters tried to follow him, but he had assumed his most stubborn air. It was aperitif hour at the Hôtel du Port, and men came to the doorway to see where he was going. He raised his hand in a brief greeting to the gendarme who was keeping guard outside the judge's house and rang the bell.

'This way . . .' Élisa said. 'The judge is waiting for you . . .'

In the library, so peaceful and so comfortable! Maigret noticed that the judge kept wringing his hands, from which the blood had drained.

'Sit down, inspector. Take off your coat, this may take a while and the room is very warm. I won't offer you any port, since I'm sure you're going to refuse it.'

A hint of bitterness in his voice.

'Not at all!'

'And what if, after what I'm about to tell you, you regret drinking with me?'

Maigret sat down in the same armchair as the other night, stretched his legs and filled his pipe.

'Do you know a Dr Janin?'

The judge really did search in his memory. It wasn't pretence.

'Janin? . . . Let me see . . . No . . . I don't think so . . .'

'He's the man you tried to throw into the sea . . .'

A strange gesture, as if to say: 'That's not what this is about. It's of no importance.'

He poured the port.

'Cheers, then!' he said. 'I haven't been trying to trick you. Before anything else, I'd like to ask you a question . . .'

He turned solemn. His face lit up beneath his light grey hair, which was still as dishevelled as a woman's.

'If anything happens and I'm not able to look after my daughter for a while, could you promise me, man to man, that no harm will come to her?'

'I assume that if . . . if what you fear does indeed come about, your daughter would be entrusted to her mother, wouldn't she?'

'When you've heard what I have to say, you'll know she can't be entrusted to her mother . . . So . . .'

'Provided it stays within the law, I'll make sure she's treated as well as possible.'

'I'm very grateful.'

He slowly finished his glass of port and walked to a drawer to look for cigarettes.

'You only smoke a pipe, don't you? Please . . .'

Finally, exhaling the first puff of smoke, he murmured:

'In these circumstances, I think, after mature reflection, that it's preferable for me to spend some time in prison . . .'

It was unexpected. At that moment, the piano could be heard above their heads. He looked up at the ceiling. When he spoke again, his voice was thick with emotion, as if he were holding back the tears.

'I killed a man, inspector . . .'

Outside, the gendarme's hobnailed shoes could be heard striking the hard stones of the pavement.

'Do you still want to finish your port?'

He took an old gold watch from his pocket and snapped open the lid.

'Midday. Not that it matters to me. But if you prefer to go and have lunch first . . . I don't dare invite you to eat here.'

He poured himself another drink, then came and sat down facing Maigret, beside the crackling fire.

6. The Two Englishwomen of Versailles

At about one o'clock, the gendarme standing guard outside the judge's house started to get nervous, and every time he passed the windows he would go closer and try to see inside.

At 1.30, he stuck his face against the window, and it took him a moment to discover two men sitting in armchairs on either side of the fireplace, their heads emerging strangely from a cloud of smoke.

At about the same hour, the clatter of forks and the murmur of women's voices could be heard from an adjoining room, and Maigret assumed it was Lise Forlacroix having lunch.

Every now and again, he would cross his legs. Some time later, he would uncross them to tap the bowl of his pipe on his heel. There were already lots of ashes on the tiled floor. What did it matter now? The judge, out of habit, stubbed out his cigarette ends in a green porcelain ashtray, and all these little white and brown ends spoke for themselves.

They talked calmly. Maigret would ask a question, raise an objection. Forlacroix would reply in a voice that was as clear and, in a way, as meticulous as his handwriting.

The ringing of the telephone at 2.15 startled them, as if they had both forgotten the outside world. Forlacroix looked inquisitively at Maigret. Was it all right if he picked up the receiver? Maigret nodded.

'Hello? . . . Yes . . . Just a moment . . . It's for you, inspector . . .'

'Hello, chief . . . Sorry to bother you . . . I don't know if I did the right thing, but I've been getting worried! . . . Nothing's happened, has it?'

The judge had sat down again and was playing with his hands and looking at the logs.

'Get me a taxi . . . Straight away, yes . . . It should be here in half an hour . . . No, nothing special . . .'

And he in his turn sat down again.

When the taxi drew up outside the front door and Méjat rang the bell, Maigret was alone in the library, walking up and down and devouring a pâté sandwich. On the table stood an almost empty bottle of old Burgundy. They had smoked so much, the air was almost unbreathable.

Méjat stood watching his chief, with a completely stupid look on his face.

'Are you arresting him? Is it over? Am I going with you?'

'You're staying here.'

'What do you want me to do?'

'Take a piece of paper. Write this down . . . Thérèse, the maid from the hotel . . . The two Hulots, Didine and her customs officer . . . Albert Forlacroix . . . We have to find Marcel Airaud whatever happens . . .'

'The others you've mentioned, shall I keep an eye on them?'

Footsteps on the stairs.

'You can go . . .'

Méjat reluctantly withdrew. The judge appeared in his hat and overcoat, looking very proper, very much the meticulous bourgeois.

'Do you mind if I phone Dr Brénéol about the convalescent home?'

Lise Forlacroix was coming and going in the room above them, along with the two maids.

'Is that you, Brénéol? . . . No, nothing serious . . . I'd just like you to tell me if there's a good convalescent home in the vicinity of La Roche-sur-Yon . . . Yes . . . The Villa Albert-Premier? . . . Just before you get to the town? . . . Thank you . . . Goodbye for now . . .'

Old Élisa came down first with two suitcases, which she carried out to the car. Then her daughter with some smaller items of luggage. Finally Lise, almost sunk inside a soft fur coat with the collar up.

It was all very quick. Lise and her father got in the back. Maigret took his seat next to the driver. From the corner of the street, Didine watched the scene. People were stopping. They had to drive all the way down the main street, past the hotel, the post office, the town hall. Curtains stirred. Children started running after the car.

In the rear-view mirror, Maigret could see Lise and her father, and he had the impression they held hands throughout the ride. Night was falling by the time they approached La Roche-sur-Yon. They had to ask several times for the address of the Villa Albert-Premier. Then to wait for the director, visit the rooms.

Everything was white, too white, like the nurses' uniforms, and the doctor's coat.

'Room 7 . . . Very well.'

Five people had gone in: Lise, a nurse, Maigret, the judge and the director.

Three of them came back out into the corridor. Lise had remained on the other side of the door with the nurse. She hadn't wept. Father and daughter hadn't kissed each other.

'In an hour's time, an inspector will come and stand guard in this corridor . . .'

Three more kilometres: the town, the gates of the prison, the register, a few formalities. By chance, no doubt, the judge and Maigret didn't have time to say goodbye to each other.

A brasserie. A fat woman at the cash desk. The railway timetable. A nice cold glass of beer.

'I'd like something to write with and a ham sandwich . . . And another glass of beer!'

He wrote an unofficial report for the prosecutor, then a few more telegrams, and caught his train just in time. From midnight until two in the morning, he had to wait at the station in Saint-Pierre.

Gare d'Orsay. At eight o'clock in the morning, freshly shaved, he left his apartment on Boulevard Richard-Lenoir. The sun was rising over Paris.

He changed buses not far from Police Headquarters and could even see the windows of his old office in the distance.

At nine o'clock, still in the sour January sunlight, he got off in Versailles and slowly, his pipe between his teeth, walked down Avenue de Paris.

From that moment, he really had the impression of being double, of living on two different planes. He was still Maigret, a detective chief inspector more or less in disgrace, exiled to Luçon. He had his hands in the pockets of Maigret's coat and he was smoking Maigret's pipe.

The setting was still Versailles that morning, and not a number of years earlier.

The avenue was calm, especially towards the end, where vast gates and high walls hide the most delightful little mansions in the world from the passer-by.

But it was a little like the reality of a film. A documentary film, for example. Images unreel on the screen. At the same time, the voice of an off-screen narrator comments on them . . .

The voice was the flat little voice of Judge Forlacroix, and it was impossible not to superimpose on the image of Versailles the image of the library in L'Aiguillon, the logs, the pipe ash on the tiled floor, the cigarette ends in the green porcelain bowl.

'We've been in Versailles for three generations. My father was a lawyer and lived all his life in the mansion on Avenue de Paris that he had inherited from his father. A white wall. A carriage entrance flanked by stone bollards. The gilded sign. Our name on a brass plate . . .'

Here it was. Maigret had located the house, but the sign was no longer there, nor the brass plate. The door was open. A manservant in a striped waistcoat had come out to beat rugs on the pavement.

'Once you get through the gate, a not very large main courtyard, with those little round cobbles you find in the great courtyard at Versailles and which are called king's stones. Grass between the cobbles. A glass canopy. High windows with small panes. Light everywhere. Across the hall, in the middle of which there's a bronze fountain, you can see a garden in the Trianon style, with its lawns and its roses. I was born there, just as my father was. I spent years there without bothering about anything except art and literature, a bit of good living, good food. I had no ambitions, and was content to become a justice of the peace . . .'

Wasn't it easier to understand him here than in the solitude of L'Aiguillon?

'A few good friends. Trips to Italy and Greece. A sufficient fortune. Some fine pieces of furniture and good books. When my father died, I was thirty-five and a bachelor . . .'

Weren't there others like Forlacroix in the surrounding houses, people who wanted nothing more than a pleasant life?

The manservant was starting to look askance at this man in his thick overcoat looking with such interest at his masters' house.

But wasn't it too early for the visit that Maigret had to pay?

Slowly, he walked back up part of the avenue, turned right, then left, looking at the names of the streets and finally stopping in front of a larger building, four storeys high, probably divided into several apartments.

'Does Mademoiselle Dochet still live here?' he asked the concierge.

'She's just now going upstairs with her shopping . . .'

He caught up with her on the first floor just as she was

turning a brass door knob. She was as antiquated as the house.

'Excuse me, mademoiselle. You are the owner of this building, aren't you? I'm looking for someone who used to live here, about twenty-five years ago . . .'

She was seventy.

'Come in. Wait while I turn off the gas in the kitchen. I don't want my milk to get burned . . .'

Stained glass panes in the windows. Crimson rugs.

'This person was a musician. A great virtuoso named Constantinesco.'

'I remember him! He lived in the apartment just above mine . . .'

So it was true. And now it was the judge's voice again that superimposed itself on the scene:

'A bohemian, who may have been almost a genius. He'd been quite successful at the beginning of his career. He'd given recitals in America and all over. He'd got married somewhere, had had a daughter, had taken her away without worrying about the mother. He'd ended up in Versailles, in an old-fashioned apartment where he gave violin lessons. Some friends brought him over one evening when we needed a viola for a chamber music session . . .'

The judge had almost blushed, looking at his white hands and adding:

'I play the piano a little.'

The old woman now declared:

'He was half mad. He'd fly into terrible tempers. You'd hear him running down the stairs yelling.'

'And his daughter?'

The woman stiffened. 'Now she's married. And well married from what I hear! To a judge, isn't it? There are those who succeed and they aren't always the most . . .'

The most what? Maigret would never know, because she had fallen silent.

There was nothing more to learn here. He knew. The judge's voice did not lie.

Valentine Constantinesco. A girl of eighteen, with an already full figure and huge eyes, who set off for Paris every morning, carrying her scores, to attend classes at the Conservatoire. She was studying the piano. At the same time, her father was teaching her the violin . . .

And here was a little judge, unmarried and Epicurean, who watched for her at the corner of the street, followed her at a distance, got on the electric train behind her.

Avenue de Paris . . . Ah! The manservant had gone back inside and closed the door behind him, that door which Valentine had crossed a few months later, in her white wedding dress . . .

Wonderful years. The birth of a boy, then a girl. Sometimes, in the summer, they would go and spend a few weeks in the old family house in L'Aiguillon . . .

'I assure you, inspector, that I'm no innocent. I'm not the kind of person who's so happy that he doesn't see what's in front of him. Many's the time I looked at her anxiously. But when you see her eyes, which can't have changed, you'll understand. As pure and clear as you could imagine. A voice like music. With her sea-green or pale blue dresses, always very light in colour, very neutral, she seemed to be straight out of a pastel.

'I didn't dare be surprised to find I'd fathered a sturdy boy with lots of hair, as coarse as a peasant. My daughter looked like her mother.

'I found out later that old Constantinesco, who was constantly hanging around the house, knew all about it.

'Wait . . . At the time I'm going to tell you about, Albert was twelve, Lise eight.

'I was supposed to go to a concert at four in the afternoon with a friend who's written several books about the history of music. He was in bed with a bout of bronchitis. I returned home.

'Maybe you'll see the house? There's a little door in the big carriage entrance. I had the key to it. Instead of coming in through the hall, I took the staircase on the right leading to the first floor where the bedrooms are. I wanted to suggest to my wife that she come with me.'

Maigret pulled on the brass button, and a big bell rang, as low-pitched as in a convent. Footsteps. The manservant, looking surprised.

'I'd like to speak to the occupants of this house, please.'

'Which of the ladies in particular?'

'Whichever you like.'

At that moment, through a ground-floor window, he saw two women, both wearing dressing gowns in glaring colours. One was smoking a cigarette at the end of a long holder, the other a tiny pipe that made Maigret smile.

'What is it, Jean?'

A strong English accent. The women were both between

forty and fifty. The room, which must once have been the Forlacroix family's large drawing room and had now been turned into a studio, was filled with easels, highly modernistic canvases, glasses, bottles, Negro and Chinese objects, a very Montparnasse-style clutter.

Maigret presented his card.

'Come in, detective chief inspector. We haven't done anything wrong, have we? My friend, Mrs Perkins. I'm Angelina Dodds. Which of us are you here to see?'

A lot of confidence, a touch of humour.

'Do you mind my asking how long you've lived here?'

'Seven years. Before us, there was an old senator who died. And before him, there was a judge, so we've been told.'

A pity that the old senator was dead! He couldn't have changed very much in this house, where Forlacroix had left him the furniture and some of the knick-knacks. Now a red and gold Chinese divan strewn with dragons stood incongruously in front of the most delicate imaginable Louis XVI pier glass.

Anyway! Two Englishwomen, eccentric obviously, crazy about painting, attracted by the prestigious setting of Versailles.

'Do you have a gardener?'

'Of course! Why?'

'Can I ask you to take me or have me taken to the garden?'

Intrigued, they both came with him. A period garden, too, trying hard to imitate the gardens of Trianon on a smaller scale.

'I tended to my rose bushes myself,' the judge had said. 'That explains why I thought of the well.'

Three wells, in the places indicated. The one in the middle, which was disused, must have contained geraniums or other flowers in summer.

'Would you mind, ladies, if I had this well pickaxed? There's bound to be some damage. I'm afraid I don't have a warrant with me, so I can't force you to agree . . .'

'Is there a treasure?' one of the two Englishwomen exclaimed with a laugh. 'Urbain! Come here with a pickaxe . . .'

In L'Aiguillon, the judge had spoken calmly, in an even voice, as if not talking about himself.

'You know what it means to catch someone in flagrante, don't you? You've seen it in hotel rooms, in more or less seedy apartments. There are cases . . . I think it all came from the fact that the man had a common face and was looking at me defiantly . . . And yet he was ridiculous, loathsome, half naked, his hair dishevelled, his left cheek streaked with lipstick . . . I killed him . . .'

'Did you carry a revolver with you?'

'No, but there was one in a chest of drawers in our bedroom. The drawer was within reach . . . I did it coldly, I admit. I was calmer than I am now. I was thinking of the children, who were due back from school . . . I found out later that he was a café singer. He wasn't handsome. He had thick greasy hair that formed a roll on the back of his neck.'

Maigret went straight up to the gardener.

'Remove the compost first. I assume it's only about twenty centimetres deep . . . And underneath . . .'

'Stones and cement.' Urbain declared.

'It's those stones and cement you need to pickaxe.'

Here the calm voice had become hallucinatory:

'I thought of the well . . . I carried the man there, his clothes, everything I found on him . . . The well wasn't very wide and, even cramming him in, I was only able to put the body in a crouching position . . . I covered it with large stones. I poured in several sacks of cement. But that's not what matters . . .'

It was about then that the gendarme had stuck his face against the window and the judge had shrugged.

'In the blink of an eye, my wife had turned into a kind of fury . . . In less than thirty minutes, inspector, I learned everything from her own mouth, the affairs she'd had before our marriage, the ruses she'd employed, her father's complicity . . . Then her many lovers, the places where she saw them . . .

'She was unrecognizable. She was literally foaming at the mouth.

'"And I really loved this one, do you hear, I loved him!" she screamed, without any concern for the children, who'd just come home and might have heard her.

'I should have called the police and told them the truth, shouldn't I? I would have been acquitted. But my son, and above all my daughter, would have spent their whole lives knowing that their mother . . .

'I did think about it, believe me, briefly. It's incredible how clearly things appear to us at such moments . . .

'I waited for night to fall. It was June. I had to wait until it was very late . . . I'm stronger than I look . . . Well, I was then . . .'

Eleven o'clock. The earth, frozen in the course of the night, was turning warm and damp in the rays of the sun.

'Well?' Maigret asked.

'See for yourself.'

The inspector leaned over. Something whitish, which the pickaxe had broken. A skull . . .

'I beg your pardon, ladies, for all this disturbance. Rest assured that you won't be bothered about it. This was a crime that took place a long time ago. I'll pay you myself until the official search has been done.'

The judge hadn't lied. He had killed a man. And for nearly fifteen years, nobody had known anything about it, except his wife, who lived on the Côte d'Azur, at the Villa des Roches-Grises in Nice, with Horace Van Usschen, a Dutch cocoa merchant.

'You will have a whisky, won't you, inspector?'

He hated whisky! Even more than talking about this case!

'I have to see the legal authorities in Versailles before midday.'

'You will come back?'

No, he wouldn't! It wasn't this crime he was dealing with, but the death, in a house in L'Aiguillon, of a certain Dr Janin. It was as if gold dust had been sprinkled over Avenue de Paris, so fine and penetrating was the sun. But now he had to be quick. A taxi was passing.

'To the Palais de Justice.'

'It's not far . . .'

'What difference does that make?'

To be announced. To see people looking at him with a mixture of scepticism and boredom. Such an old case! Was it really necessary to . . .

He had lunch alone, a sauerkraut, at the Brasserie Suisse. He read the newspaper without reading it.

'Waiter! Can you get me number 41 at La Roche-sur-Yon . . . Priority, police . . . One moment . . . Can you also get me the prison . . .'

The beer was good, the choucroute acceptable, very acceptable, and he asked for a second pair of sausages. It wasn't very Louis XIV, but too bad!

'Hello? . . . Yes . . . She's been quiet? . . . That's excellent . . . What's that? . . . She asked for a piano? . . . Then hire her one . . . But of course! . . . I'll vouch for it . . . The father will pay anything that's needed . . . Only, if you ever leave the corridor or if she gets out through the window . . .'

At the prison, nothing to report. At eleven o'clock, Judge Forlacroix had had a visit from his lawyer, and they had conversed calmly for half an hour.

7. 'Ask the Inspector . . .'

It was a joy, at eight in the morning, to walk down the overly narrow stairs, whose pitch-pine banisters shone in the sunlight, and find the main room of the hotel empty, then go and take your seat at your usual table, which was already laid with a heavy porcelain bowl, homemade sausage and shrimps caught that morning.

'Thérèse!' he called as he sat down. 'My coffee . . .'

It was the hotelier's wife who brought it.

'Thérèse has gone to the butcher's.'

'Tell me, madame. I don't see anybody in the harbour, even though the tide is low. Are people here scared of the cold?'

'It's the neap tide,' she replied.

'What's that?'

'They can't go to the mussel fields when there's a neap tide.'

'In other words, the mussel farmers only work half of the time?'

'Oh, no! Most of them have land, marshes, livestock . . .'

Even Méjat received a warm welcome, in spite of his brilliantine and his ridiculously garish green scarf.

'Sit down. Eat. And tell me what you discovered when you visited that poor old woman.'

He was referring to Marcel's mother. To be honest,

Maigret had been happy to offload this mission on to Méjat.

'An old rustic house, I suppose? Old furniture that smells of times gone by. A grandfather clock with a brass pendulum that moves slowly . . .'

'Nothing like that, chief. The house is repainted every year. The old door has been replaced by a modern door covered in imitation wrought iron. The furniture comes from a department store on Boulevard Barbès.'

'She started by offering you a drink . . .'

'Yes.'

'And you simply couldn't refuse . . .'

Poor Méjat wondered what sin he had committed by accepting a glass of the local plum brandy.

'Don't blush. I was thinking of someone else.'

Maybe of himself, when he'd drunk in the judge's house?

'There are people who are able to refuse and others who aren't. You went to see that old lady in order to find out something that could be used against her son, and the first thing you did was drink her plum brandy . . . I think the judge is a man capable of refusing. Refusing anything! Even himself! . . . Don't try to understand . . . Did she cry?'

'You know, she's almost as tall and as strong as her son. She blustered at first, then got indignant. She said that if this went on she'd go and see a lawyer. I asked her if her son had been away recently. I got the impression she hesitated.

'"I think he went to Niort on business."

'"Are you sure it was Niort? Did he spend the night there?"

'"I can't remember."

'"How is it possible you can't remember, when you live alone together in the same house? Would you agree to showing me the bedrooms? I haven't brought a warrant, but if you refuse . . ."

'We went up to the first floor. Up there, the house was old, with old furniture, like you said before, huge wardrobes and sideboards, and photographic enlargements.

'"What suit does your son wear when he goes to town?"

'She took it out. A blue serge suit. I searched the pockets. I found this bill from a hotel in Nantes. Look at the date.

'It's the 5th of January, a few days before Dr Janin arrived in L'Aiguillon.'

'So you didn't regret the glass of plum brandy?' Maigret asked, standing up to greet the telegraph boy.

He came back to the table with several telegrams, which he put down in front of him, although, as usual, he was in no hurry to open them.

'By the way, do you know why old Didine and her husband hate the judge so much? I looked for a complicated reason, and yet the truth is quite simple, as simple as this village, as simple as that lighthouse you can see over there in the sun . . . When the Hulots retired and saw the judge had settled in L'Aiguillon, Didine went to see him and reminded him that they'd known each other as children. She offered him their services, herself as cook, her husband as gardener. Forlacroix, who must have known what she was like, refused. That's all . . .'

He tore the strip from a telegram, read it, and handed it to Méjat.

Naval volunteer Marcel Airaud served his term on board destroyer *Vengeur*.

'But seeing as how the judge has confessed . . . !' Méjat exclaimed.

'Oh, has he confessed?'

'It's in all the newspapers.'

'And you still believe what the newspapers say, do you?'

He was patient enough to wait for ten o'clock, doing virtually nothing, wandering among the moored boats, looking at the house, and the only reason he twice went back to the hotel to have a quick drink was because it was really cold.

He smiled when he saw the two cars arrive one behind the other, because this respect for form was touching, even comical. The two men arriving from La Roche-sur-Yon so early in the morning were old friends, who had known each other since school days. It would have been more pleasant for them to have made the journey in a single car. But one was the examining magistrate dealing with the case in L'Aiguillon, the other the lawyer chosen by Judge Forlacroix. In such circumstances, they had debated for a long time, the previous day, the question of whether or not it was appropriate . . .

They both shook Maigret's hand. The lawyer, Maître Courtieux, was a middle-aged man who was considered the best lawyer in the region.

'My client told me he's given you all the keys.'

Maigret jangled them in his pocket, and all three headed for the house, which was still guarded by a gendarme. The examining magistrate remarked casually, although clearly concerned to show that nothing escaped him:

'Strictly speaking, the seals should have been put on . . . Anyway! Since it's Monsieur Forlacroix himself who gave the inspector the keys and asked him to . . .'

The surprising thing was seeing Maigret go in and make himself at home, hang his coat on the stand, knowing exactly where it was, and walk into the library.

'As we're going to be a while, I think I'll light the fire . . .'

It wasn't without a certain emotion that he saw again the two armchairs by the fire, the pipe ash that hadn't been swept away, the cigarette ends.

'Please make yourselves comfortable, gentlemen.'

'My client told me,' the lawyer began, a little upset: "Ask the inspector . . ."'

'So it's you, inspector, who will tell us what he did after killing that man and walling him up, so to speak, in his well . . .'

'You go first, your honour,' Maigret said to the examining magistrate, as if he were the master of the house. 'Please note that I'm not hoping to find anything remarkable. The reason I've asked for this search is rather to help me reconstruct the life of Judge Forlacroix over the last few years . . .

'See with what sure taste all this furniture has been chosen and how each item, each knick-knack, too, is in its place.'

Forlacroix hadn't left Versailles immediately. He had written his wife quite a large cheque and thrown her out, simply, coldly.

Maigret could imagine him very well: small, thin, icy, with his halo of hair and his precise, nervous fingers. He wasn't, as the inspector had said that morning, the kind of person who accepts anything he doesn't want to accept. Didine knew about that: despite the years that had passed, she hadn't forgotten how calmly and coldly her proposition had been rejected. Not even rejected – ignored!

'She didn't try to stay with you and her children?' Maigret had insisted when they were both sitting by the fire.

Of course she had! There had been ugly scenes! She had grovelled to him. Then, for months, she had written. She had begged, threatened.

'I never replied. One day, I found out she was living on the Côte d'Azur with a Dutchman.'

He had sold the house in Versailles. He had moved to L'Aiguillon. And then . . .

'Can you feel the atmosphere of this house, where everything exudes comfort and easy living?' Maigret sighed. 'For years, a man spent his days here, watching his two children and wondering if they were his . . . For his part, the boy, as he grew up, tried to understand the mystery surrounding him, asked questions about his mother, about his birth . . .'

He had just opened the door of a room, where toys of all kinds were still in their place, with, in a corner, a pupil's desk in light-coloured oak.

Further on, there was Albert's old room, still with clothes in the wardrobe. Elsewhere, a cupboard was full of Lise Forlacroix's dolls.

'At the age of seventeen or eighteen,' Maigret went on,

'Albert started, God knows why, to hate his father. He couldn't understand why his father kept his sister locked up. That was when Lise had just had her first attack.

'It was about this time also that Albert discovered one of his mother's old letters, a letter written soon after the drama . . . Here . . . It must be in this writing desk . . . I have the key . . .'

It wasn't only the key to the Louis XIV desk that he seemed to have, but the key to all these characters who had clashed with each other throughout the years. He was smoking his pipe. The magistrate and the lawyer followed him. To touch certain things, to tackle certain subjects, he drew on the kind of tact that might not have been expected from this big man with his thick hands.

'You can add it to the file,' he said without reading it. 'I know what it says. She threatens her husband with prison. Albert demanded to know what had happened. Forlacroix refused to tell him. From that point on, they lived like strangers. After his military service, Albert wanted to live as he pleased, but a strange kind of curiosity kept him in L'Aiguillon, and he settled down here as a mussel farmer. You've seen him. Despite his physique, he's a restless, violent man, who could easily become a rebel. As for the girl . . .'

The doorbell rang. Maigret went to open it. It was Méjat with a telegram; he would have liked to come in, but his chief didn't even suggest it. When Maigret came back upstairs, he announced:

'She's replied to my telegram. She's coming.'

'Who?'

'Madame Forlacroix. She left Nice at midday yesterday by car.'

It was impressive to observe Maigret. In fact, a curious phenomenon was taking place. As he came and went in this house that wasn't his, as he evoked lives he hadn't lived, he was no longer entirely the heavy, placid, rough-hewn Maigret. Without his realizing it, there was a little of Forlacroix in the way he moved, the way he spoke. The two men could not have been more dissimilar and yet, at certain moments, it was so striking that the lawyer was quite bothered by it.

'When I visited the house the first time, Lise was in bed . . . Look. This bedside lamp was on . . . Forlacroix loved his daughter. He loved her, and that made him suffer because, in spite of everything, he still had his doubts. What proved that she was his child and not the child of some passing lover like the singer with the greasy hair?

'He also loved her because she wasn't like anyone else, because she needed him, because she was a tender and impulsive young animal.

'Outside her attacks, I imagine she was like a six-year-old, her whims, her charms . . .

'Her father consulted specialists from all over. I can tell you this, gentlemen: young girls like Lise don't usually live beyond the age of sixteen or seventeen. When they survive, the attacks become more frequent, leaving them depressed and distrustful.

'The locals may have exaggerated, but we can be sure that several men, two at least, took advantage of her before Marcel Airaud.

'When Marcel came along . . .'

'Excuse me!' the examining magistrate said. 'I haven't yet questioned the prisoner. Is he claiming that he knew nothing about Marcel Airaud's nocturnal visits to his daughter?'

Maigret looked for a moment through the window, then turned.

'No.'

An embarrassed silence.

'So he . . .' the magistrate resumed.

And the lawyer was wondering already how he would present such a monstrous thing to a jury in La Roche-sur-Yon.

'He knew . . .' Maigret retorted. 'The doctors he'd consulted were all of the same opinion: "Marry her off! It's the only chance to . . ."'

'Between marrying her off and allowing an individual like Airaud . . .'

'Do you think, your honour, that a girl suffering from such a condition is easy to marry off? Forlacroix preferred to turn a blind eye. He made inquiries about Airaud. He was able to discover that he was quite a decent young man, in spite of his affair with Thérèse . . . I'll tell you about that another time . . . I'll tell you then that he also had his doubts as to whether Thérèse's child was his. Since then she's been plaguing him. Airaud was really in love with Lise. So in love that he was ready to marry her in spite of everything . . .'

He paused, tapped the bowl of his pipe against his heel and announced in a soft voice:

'They were due to be married soon . . .'

'What did you say?'

'That Marcel and Lise were due to be married in two months' time . . . If you knew Forlacroix better, you'd understand. A man who has the patience to live for years and years as he has lived. He watched Marcel for a long time. One day, as Airaud was passing the house, the door opened . . .

'Forlacroix stood in the doorway and said to the scared young man: "Wouldn't you like to come in for a moment?"'

Mechanically, Maigret proceeded to rewind a clock that had stopped.

'I know that's what happened because I've also sat next to him by the fire. He must have spoken very calmly. He poured the port carefully into the crystal glasses and said . . . He said what he needed to say . . . The truth about Lise . . .

'Airaud was flabbergasted and didn't know what to reply. He asked for a few days to think it over. It was yes, without any doubt. Do you know any simple, solid people like him, your honour? Have you ever watched them at the fair? Have you heard them negotiating a deal?

'What I think is that Airaud remembered the former doctor on the *Vengeur*, with whom he may once have been friendly . . . He went to Nantes . . .'

A car horn. Long, unexpected sounds. Through the window, they saw a luxury car, driven by a liveried chauffeur, who got out and went to open the rear door.

Maigret and his companions were in a room which was something like Lise's boudoir, the room where the piano was. All three followed the scene through the window.

'Horace Van Usschen!' Maigret announced, pointing to an old man who was the first passenger to get out, with abrupt, automatic movements, as if his joints had not been oiled.

Some villagers had gathered at the corner of the street. Van Usschen was indeed a sight for sore eyes, with his light flannel suit, his white shoes, his vast check overcoat and his white cloth cap. Dressed like that, he would have caused no surprise on the Côte d'Azur, but was a somewhat unusual sight in L'Aiguillon, where the only tourists you saw during the summer months were people on very modest incomes.

He was as thin and wrinkled as Rockefeller, whom he somewhat resembled. He reached his hand inside the car. And it was then that a huge woman appeared, clad in furs, who looked the house up and down. She spoke to the chauffeur, who came and rang the doorbell.

'If you agree with me, gentlemen, we'll leave the Dutchman outside. At least for the moment . . .'

He went to open the door and saw at first glance that the judge had not lied, that Valentine Forlacroix, née Constantinesco, had been beautiful, that she still had wonderful eyes and sensual lips which, in spite of the sagging at the corners, recalled Lise's.

'Well, I'm here,' she announced. 'Come, Horace.'

'I'm sorry, madame, but for the moment I'd like you to come in on your own. That may be best for you, too, don't you think?'

Irritably, Horace got back in the car, wrapped himself

in a blanket and sat there motionless, ignoring the children staring at him through the windows.

'You know the house. If you like, we can go in the library. There's a fire there . . .'

'I wonder in what way that man's crime is any concern of mine!' she protested as she entered the room. 'He may be my husband, but we haven't lived together for many years, and what he gets up to these days doesn't interest me.'

The magistrate and the lawyer had now also come downstairs.

'The examining magistrate here will tell you that we're not concerned about what he gets up to these days, but what you both got up to when you were still living together . . .'

A strong perfume gradually permeated the room. With a heavily ringed hand, the nails blood red, Valentine Forlacroix opened a cigarette box that was on the table and looked for matches.

Maigret reached an already lighted one to her.

The examining magistrate thought it time to intervene and play his role.

'I am sure you are not unaware, madame, that the law may pursue as an accessory not just a person who has participated in a crime, but also one who has witnessed a crime without reporting it to the authorities . . .'

She was strong! Forlacroix hadn't lied! She took the time to puff at her cigarette. Her mink coat open over a black silk dress adorned with a diamond brooch, she walked up and down the vast room, stopped by the fire, bent down, seized the tongs and straightened one of the logs.

When she turned, she was no longer playacting. She was ready for a fight. Her eyes had lost their brightness but had gained in sharpness. Her lips were tense.

'Very well!' she said, sitting down on a chair and placing one elbow on the table. 'I'm ready to listen to you . . . As for you, inspector, I shan't congratulate you on the trap you set me.'

'What trap?' the examining magistrate said in surprise, turning to Maigret.

'It wasn't a trap,' Maigret grunted, putting his pipe out with his thumb. 'I telegraphed Madame and asked her to come here and explain the visit she paid her husband about a month ago . . . In fact, your honour, that's the question I'd like you to ask first, if you don't mind . . .'

'Did you hear that, madame? I must inform you that in the absence of my clerk, this interview is not official and that Maître Courtieux here is your husband's lawyer.'

She blew out smoke with a scornful air and shrugged. 'I came to ask him for a divorce!' she said.

'Why now and not before?'

The phenomenon that Forlacroix had talked of now came about. In an instant, this diamond-bedecked woman became embarrassingly vulgar.

'Because Van Usschen is seventy-eight, don't you see?' she admitted crudely.

'And you'd like to get married?'

'He's been wanting to for the past six months, ever since his nephew came to scrounge money from him after losing hundreds of thousands of francs at roulette . . .'

'So you came here. Did your husband receive you?'

'In the passage.'

'What did he say?'

'That he didn't know me and so there was no reason to get a divorce.'

Maigret would gladly have clapped, so typical of Forlacroix was that answer. He wrote a few words in pencil on a piece of paper, which he passed to the magistrate, because from now on he had to step aside in favour of the latter.

'What did you do after that?'

'I went back to Nice.'

'Just a moment! Didn't you see anyone else in L'Aiguillon?'

'Who do you mean?'

'Your son, for example.'

A hate-filled look at Maigret.

'I see the man just can't keep his mouth shut . . . I did meet my son, as it happens.'

'How did you meet him?'

'I went to his house.'

'Did he recognize you after so many years?'

She shrugged.

'What does it matter? I told him he wasn't Forlacroix's son.'

'Are you sure of that?'

'Can you ever be sure? I told him I wanted to get a divorce, that my husband was refusing, that he was a cruel man, that he had a lot on his conscience and that if he, Albert, could get him to agree to a divorce . . . '

'In other words, you got your son on your side. Did you offer him money?'

'He didn't want any.'

'Did he promise to help you?'

She nodded.

'Did you tell him about the old crime?'

'No. I just told him that, if I wanted, Forlacroix would go to prison for a long time.'

'Did you write to him after that?'

'To ask him if he'd got anywhere.'

'Have you ever heard of a Dr Janin?'

'No, never!'

The magistrate looked inquisitively at Maigret, who murmured:

'If Madame is tired, maybe we could let her go and have lunch? I have the impression that Monsieur Van Usschen is getting bored in the car.'

'Am I under arrest?'

'Not yet,' the magistrate declared. 'I simply ask you to remain at the disposal of the authorities. If you'd like to give me an address in La Roche-sur-Yon, for example.'

'Very well! Hôtel des Deux Cerfs. I think it's the best one there.'

They all stood up. As she went out, she smiled at both the magistrate and the lawyer but had to restrain herself from sticking her tongue out or making a face at Maigret, who joyfully relit his pipe.

8. *The Potato Eaters*

'*Tierce* . . . That's trumps . . .'

'Not worth anything, my friend . . . Fifty . . .'

'Let me see! In case your fifty's full of holes . . .'

What time was it? The cheap clock on the wall had stopped. The lights had been on for some time now . . . It was hot. The little glasses had been filled three or four times and a smell of marc mingled with the smell of the pipes.

'Too bad! I'm playing trumps!' Maigret said, laying down a card.

'That's the best thing you can do, Inspector. Even if you have a nine after it . . .'

It was their fourth or fifth game. Maigret was smoking, tipped back slightly on his chair. His partner was the hotelier, and the other two were fishermen, including old Bariteau, the eel fisher.

Inspector Méjat sat astride a chair, following the game.

'I knew perfectly well you had a nine . . .'

'Tell me, Méjat. Do you remember the name of the pathologist?'

'I wrote it down.'

'I want you to phone him. Ask him if he can determine roughly how long before his death the man ate for the last time. And if it was a full meal. Do you understand?'

'Who was it who had a fifty? . . . And thirty-six . . .'

The owner was counting. Maigret seemed buried up to his neck in a kind of warm, mundane state of bliss, and if anyone had suddenly asked him what he was thinking about, he would have been surprised himself.

An old memory! From the time of the Bonnot case, when he was thin and wore a long pointed moustache and a little beard, false stiff collars ten centimetres high and top hats.

'You know, my dear Maigret,' his chief at the time – Detective Chief Inspector Xavier Guichard, later to become commissioner of the Police Judiciaire – had said to him, 'all these stories about intuition' (the newspapers had been talking about his infallible intuition) 'are fine for entertaining the public. In a criminal case, what matters before anything else is to store away the fact, or the two or three facts, you're absolutely certain about, because, whatever happens, they'll stay solid, and you can use them as a foundation.

'After that, all you have to do is push ahead, slowly and surely, the way you'd push a wheelbarrow. It's a question of expertise, and what people call intuition is nothing but chance . . .'

As strange as it might seem, it was because of that memory that he had agreed to play cards, much to Méjat's astonishment.

After Valentine Forlacroix and the Dutchman had driven off in their car, the other two cars had left, those of the examining magistrate and the lawyer. Maigret had stood alone for a moment, seemingly helpless, in the middle of the street. Forlacroix was in prison. His daughter Lise was in a clinic. Before leaving, the examining magistrate had placed seals on the house.

He had left satisfied, as if carrying off his booty. All this belonged to him now! It was he, in his office at the Palais de Justice in La Roche-sur-Yon, who was going to proceed with the interviews, with bringing the witnesses face to face . . .

'Let's go!' Maigret had muttered as he walked back into the hotel.

Why was he so queasy? Wasn't it always like this? And wasn't this feeling, a feeling that resembled jealousy, quite ridiculous?

'What do we do now, chief?'

'Where's the list I dictated to you?'

. . . Didine and her husband . . . Marcel Airaud . . . Thérèse . . . Albert Forlacroix . . .

'Who shall we start with?'

He had started with a game of cards.

'Can I play a lower card here?'

'Only in trumps . . . What about in Paris?'

'It depends . . . Anyway, here's my eight . . .'

After a while, leaving his partner to count the points, he had taken a pencil and a notebook from his pocket, even though he never took notes, and had written, pressing down so hard that he had broken the lead:

Doctor Janin arrived in L'Aiguillon on Tuesday at between four fifteen and four thirty.

That was the first sure-fire element, as Xavier Guichard would have said. And after that? He almost added that the very same Janin had been killed in the judge's house that night. But that was no longer certain. After three days, the pathologist had only been able to pinpoint the time of death to within a few hours. And nothing proved . . .

On Wednesday morning, Janin's body is lying on the floor in the fruitery of the judge's house.

'Hearts are trumps . . . Are you playing?' someone asked him, surprised to see him staring into space.

'Hearts are fine! . . . Whose turn is it?'

The hotelier respectfully refrained from saying the traditional: 'The idiot who's asking . . .'

Since then, Maigret had glanced from time to time at those two little sentences that constituted the only sure-fire elements of the case.

Méjat could be heard telephoning under the stairs, and, whenever he spoke on the telephone, he assumed a horrible head voice.

'Well?'

'The doctor had to reread his report. According to the contents of the stomach, a normal meal. There were quite strong traces of alcohol . . .'

Méjat couldn't understand why Maigret looked so pleased. The inspector sat so far back in his chair that he almost lost his balance and had to hold on to the table.

'Well, well,' he said after examining his cards, 'so the rascal had something to eat!'

It might not be much. And yet . . . Janin hadn't had dinner at the Hôtel du Port, nor at the inn opposite, and there was nowhere else to eat in L'Aiguillon.

'*Tierce* . . .'

'How high?'

'Kings . . . By the way, doesn't young Forlacroix have a lorry?'

'Yes, he does, but it's been under repair for the last two weeks.'

No motorist had reported driving Janin anywhere by car. So if he had eaten . . .

'Méjat . . . Run to the butcher.' He turned to the hotelier. 'Tell me . . . There is only one butcher here, isn't there?'

'And he only slaughters once a week.'

'Ask him if that Tuesday, between four and seven, anyone came in for a good cut of meat.'

'Who?'

'Anyone.'

Méjat put on his overcoat and left with a sigh. As the door opened and closed again, it let in cold air, which you could feel gliding between your legs. Thérèse was sitting by the stove, knitting. No sooner had the door closed than it opened again. It was Méjat, making signals at the inspector.

'What do you want?'

'Can I have a word, chief?'

'One moment . . . Trumps! . . . Clubs! . . . And you won't take this ace of diamonds away from me . . . You've lost, gentlemen!'

Then, to Méjat:

'What is it?'

'Didine's outside. She's asking for you to come straight away. Apparently it's urgent.'

'Give me my hat and coat, Thérèse . . . You, take my place for a moment . . .'

He lit his pipe before going out. The night was pitch black. It was freezing cold. Only a few lights could be seen in the street, and in the window of the grocery, covered in transparent advertisements. Didine's little figure somehow hitched itself to Maigret.

'Come with me. Let's not walk together. You just have to follow me, so that they don't know I'm leading you.'

She was carrying a half-filled sack and in her other hand she held a pruning knife, like those old ladies who go out to cut grass for their rabbits. After a while, they passed Albert Forlacroix's house, and a figure moved in the shadows; the gendarme on guard gave a military salute.

Every now and again, Didine turned to make sure that Maigret was following her. Suddenly, she disappeared, as if sucked into the black void that formed a gap between two houses. He turned into this gap. An icy hand touched his.

'Careful! There's barbed wire.'

By day, the place was probably ordinary enough. In the darkness, led on by this strange little witch with her sack and her sickle, Maigret was finding it hard to perceive the layout of the place. He caught his feet on oyster shells, then a strong smell of dustbins struck his nostrils.

'Step over. There's a little fence.'

Frozen cabbages. They were in a vegetable garden

behind the houses. There were other, similar gardens, separated by old trellises. Something living stirred: rabbits in a hutch.

'I'd come to get some grass for my rabbits,' she said, still walking.

The village, in fact, had only one row of houses all along the street. Behind these houses were the vegetable gardens, then there was a ditch, filled with seawater at high tide, and finally the marshes, stretching to infinity.

'Don't make any noise. Don't say a word. Careful where you put your feet.'

She didn't let go of his hand. A few moments later, she was walking alongside a whitewashed wall.

He made out a figure near a dimly lit window. He recognized Justin Hulot, who placed a finger over his lips.

He would have been hard put to say what he was expecting. In any case, not the spectacle he had before his eyes a moment later, as peaceful and calm as a scene in one of those chromos that stay on the walls of rustic houses for generations.

Hulot had withdrawn to make room for him at the window. The latter being a little low for him, he had to bend down. Through the glass, he could see a stable lantern standing on a barrel, giving out a yellowish light.

Maigret had already calculated that they must be just behind Albert Forlacroix's house. What they discovered was the interior of a shed at the end of the backyard, which served as a storehouse, the kind you find in all country areas: empty barrels, saucepans, rusty old tools, sacks, crates, bottles . . .

In the fireplace, where the food for the animals was probably cooked, and a pig roasted at Christmas, a few logs were burning.

Two men were sitting by the fire, one on a crate, the other on an upended basket. They both wore high rubber boots pulled down at the knee, which always reminded Maigret of the Three Musketeers.

They were both tall, strong and young. Two strangely dressed giants. Of course they were merely wearing the traditional costume of the mussel farmer, but in this light, the two men were rather reminiscent of figures out of some painting in a museum.

One of them took a cigarette from his pocket and held it out to his companion, who grabbed a brand from the fire.

They were speaking. You could see their lips moving, but unfortunately it was impossible to hear a sound.

One of the two men, the one who had taken out the cigarette and who now took another for himself, was Albert Forlacroix. The second, sitting right up against the fire, was Marcel Airaud, barely recognizable because of a growth of blond beard already several centimetres thick.

Didine's thin body brushed against Maigret and she whispered:

'They were already there an hour ago when I looked in for the first time. It was just starting to get dark. Young Forlacroix left for a moment to go and look for potatoes . . .'

He didn't understand what potatoes had to do with anything, and the remark struck him as ridiculous.

'I didn't want to go into the hotel. I knocked lightly at

the window, but you were playing cards and didn't even notice.'

What a strange little mouse! So she had trotted home and sent her husband to keep guard!

Was it only chance that had led her to take a look inside Albert Forlacroix's property while out cutting grass for her rabbits? If not, what other train of thought could have brought her to this place? That wasn't the least troubling aspect of the matter. Her husband had moved two or three metres away and was waiting.

'I suspected he would come back . . .' she resumed.

'And that he'd see Albert Forlacroix?'

'Shhh . . .'

Maigret wasn't good at keeping his voice low, so it was best for him not to say anything.

'Are you going to arrest the two of them?' Didine whispered.

He didn't reply. He didn't move. Behind them, the Baleines lighthouse turned in the sky at a regular pace, and occasionally a cow mooed out on the marshes. The game must still be going on at the Hôtel du Port, and presumably Thérèse was getting worried by Maigret's absence.

As for the two men . . . Maigret hadn't noticed before how similar they were physically. In both cases, their line of work, the salt water, the spindrift, the sea air, had turned their skin deep pink and bleached their hair . . .

They were both heavy, with the heaviness of people who are constantly struggling with the patient forces of nature.

They were smoking. They were talking slowly. Their

eyes were fixed on the fire, and after a while Marcel stirred something in the ashes with the end of a piece of iron, his face expressing a simple joy.

He said something to Albert, who rose and went to the low door, bending to walk through it. When he returned after a short time, he was holding two big glasses, which he went and filled straight from a barrel in the corner.

White wine! Never before in his life had Maigret had such a yearning for white wine, so delicious did this one seem. As for the potatoes . . . Because, sure enough, there were potatoes . . .

It brought back childhood memories, the kind of engravings you find in books by Fenimore Cooper or Jules Verne. They were in France, in the very heart of a French village. And at the same time, they were a long way away. The two men could have been trappers, or castaways on a desert island. Their work clothes were of no particular period. Marcel's thick, shapeless beard added to the illusion.

And it was large, hot, blackened potatoes he was removing from the ashes with his piece of iron, potatoes whose charred skin he cracked between his big fingers. The white steaming flesh appeared, and he bit into it greedily.

Then his companion stood up, almost touching the ceiling with his head. He took a knife from his pocket and cut two sausages from the string of them drying above the fireplace.

'What are they doing?' Didine whispered.

He didn't reply. He would have given a lot to share that improvised meal, those potatoes cooked under ash, those sausages browned by time, that wine that appeared so refreshing!

The most troubling thing was the ease, the calm of those two strong men, who were far from suspecting that their gestures and lip movements were being spied upon.

What could they be saying to each other? There they were, confident in themselves, confident in one another. Almost crouching, they ate, each with a knife he had pulled from his pocket, in the style of peasants and sailors. They talked unhurriedly. From time to time, they would utter a few words, then let silence fall again.

'Aren't you arresting them?'

Maigret gave a start, because something had just brushed against his leg. It was only a dog, a little hunting dog, not much more than a puppy, which must belong to one of the neighbours and was silently rubbing up against him.

'Justin!' Didine called.

She pointed to the dog, which might bark at any moment. Hulot took the animal by the scruff of its neck and walked away with it.

There was no gaiety, though, on the other side of the window. No gaiety, but no anxiety either. A kind of ponderous tranquillity. Albert got up to get some more sausages, and for a moment, as he turned in his direction, Maigret thought that he had seen him through the glass. But he hadn't.

Finally, they wiped their lips and lit more cigarettes. Airaud yawned. How long was it, hunted as he was by the police, since he had last slept in peace? He scraped his teeth with the point of his knife and rested his head against the wall.

Once again, young Forlacroix disappeared. This time he was absent for longer, and Maigret started to get worried. At last he opened the door with his foot. He was heavily laden. He had a mattress folded in two on his head and some blankets and a pillow under his arm. Marcel helped him. They even displayed an unexpected concern for cleanliness. Before laying the mattress on the ground, Airaud went to fetch an old stable broom from a corner and gave the beaten-earth floor a bit of a sweep.

Hulot had got rid of the dog and come back to his post, where he was waiting patiently.

'Aren't you arresting them?' Didine whispered again, shivering.

Airaud took off his oilskin jacket and sat down on the floor to remove his boots. You could see him get rid of his socks and rub his swollen feet for a long time, with a strange kind of solicitude. Albert asked him a question. Was he offering him hot water to bathe his feet? Maigret would have sworn he was. Marcel stretched one more time and finally lay down full-length on the mattress with such a loud sigh you had the impression you could hear it from outside.

Albert Forlacroix took the stable lantern, glanced around him and frowned as he looked at the window. Had he forgotten about it? No, he was making sure! He knew it looked out on nothing but the marshes.

A curious gesture . . . A pat on his companion's shock of hair . . . Huge and heavy, carrying his lantern at arm's length, he walked away and closed the door behind him . . .

'Can we get out this way?' Maigret asked Didine after

drawing her aside. She pointed to a low wall dividing For-lacroix's yard.

Leaving Hulot on guard, he again waded through oyster shells, dustbins and shards of broken glass, abandoned Didine in the street and walked to the police station.

When he had dispatched a gendarme to take Hulot's place, he went out into the street once again. Didine was still there, with her sack half full of grass and her sickle. He had the feeling she was looking at him with a sardonic air.

'So what do you think? It seems to me that without old Didine . . . How many of your gendarmes did you send off to track him down? . . . Gendarmes! . . .' She laughed scornfully. 'But me! Nobody bothers to come and see me, even though I could . . .'

'Go home!' he advised her. 'Tonight. Or tomorrow.'

'Or on Trinity Sunday!' she said, without any illusions. 'Come, Justin. I bet they'll still find a way not to put them in prison . . .'

The gendarme outside Albert Forlacroix's house was no longer in his patch of shadow, but in the middle of the street.

'Has he come out?' Maigret asked.

'There . . . You see that figure after the third street lamp? . . . That's him . . . He's just going into the hotel . . .'

Maigret followed him in a few minutes later. The game of cards was still going on. Méjat, as was to be expected, was discussing all the hands.

'I tell you that as long as you make an indirect call . . . At last, inspector . . . If I play hearts when . . .'

Albert Forlacroix was sitting all alone at a long table where there was enough room for ten people. He was following the game from a distance. Thérèse had placed a bottle of white wine in front of him, but he was in no hurry to drink it.

'Damn!' Maigret grunted, remembering the wine drawn from the barrel, the potatoes, the sausages.

'Do you want your seat back, chief?'

'Not now . . . Carry on . . .'

He hadn't taken his overcoat off. He was in two minds as he watched Albert, who sat there with his big legs stretched in front of him.

Did he feel up to it? Did he have the will for it? If he started, he'd have to see it through, come what may. The wall clock hadn't advanced. He looked at his watch. It was seven o'clock. Thérèse was laying the table.

Should he eat first? Or should he . . .

'Give me a half-bottle of white wine, Thérèse!' he ordered.

He was sure, though, that it was nothing like the white wine the others had drunk!

Albert Forlacroix was watching him pensively.

'Tell me, Méjat . . .'

'Yes, chief . . . Sorry . . . I forgot to call my *tierce*.'

'It's fine!'

'Did you see the butcher?'

'He's just been in. I asked him the question. He doesn't remember. He claims he'd remember if anyone had asked for a good cut of meat at that hour.'

He was going round in circles. He was still in two minds.

He went down the two steps that separated him from the kitchen and lifted the lids of the saucepans.

'What have you made us for dinner?' he asked the hotelier's wife.

'Calves' liver à la bourgeoise. I hope you like it? I didn't think of asking you.'

That made up his mind for him. He hated calves' liver in all its forms.

'Méjat, when you've finished, come over to the town hall . . . Is the fire on?'

'It was earlier.'

At last, he went and stood in front of Albert Forlacroix. 'How about you and me having a little chat? Not here. In my office. I hope you've had dinner?'

Albert stood up without a word.

'Let's go, then.'

And the two of them set off into the night.

9. The 'Singing Session'

Someone from Quai des Orfèvres, a Lucas or a Janvier, wouldn't have needed to watch Maigret for a long time to understand. Even his back spoke volumes! Had it grown rounder? Were his shoulders sagging? Whatever the case, if they had seen that back looming in the long corridor of the Police Judiciaire, and if Maigret had shown a man into his office without a word, the inspectors would have looked at each other.

'Hmm! There's a witness who knows when he goes in . . .'

And they wouldn't have been surprised if, two or three hours later, they had seen a waiter from the Brasserie Dauphine bringing sandwiches and beer.

Here, there was nobody to watch Maigret and his companion as they walked in the darkness of the street.

'Would you mind waiting a second?'

Maigret walked into the little grocery, which was full of strange smells, and bought some shag and matches.

'Give me a packet of blue cigarettes, too . . . Two packets! . . .'

He could see the sweets he had liked most when he was a child, all stuck together in a jar, but he didn't dare buy any. As they walked, Albert Forlacroix remained silent, visibly trying to look as detached as possible.

The gate, the courtyard of the town hall, then, in the office, a blast of warm air, the stove glowing red in the dark.

'Come in, Forlacroix. Make yourself at home.'

Maigret switched on the lights, took off his hat and coat, refilled the stove, walked around the room two or three times, and as he did so, a kind of glimmer of anxiety could be seen passing over his face. He came and went, glanced here and there, moved objects about, smoked and muttered, as if expecting something that hadn't yet come.

And that something was the feeling of being at ease in his own skin, as he usually put it, glad to avoid the word 'inspiration'.

'Sit down. You can smoke.'

He waited for Forlacroix to do what many country people do: take a cigarette directly from an open packet in his jacket pocket. He lit it for him, then, before sitting down in his turn, remembered the window of that shed; he glanced at the window here in the town hall, thought of closing the shutter but couldn't get the pane open, and finally contented himself with lowering the dusty blind.

'Well, now!' he sighed, sitting down with evident satisfaction. 'What do you have to say for yourself, Forlacroix?'

The 'singing session', as they called it at Quai des Orfèvres, was about to begin. Albert was suspicious. His body tilted backwards a little because his legs were too long for his chair. He looked at Maigret with no attempt to hide his resentment.

'Was it you who sent for my mother?' he asked after a moment's silence.

So he had seen her, either when she had got out of the car or when she had got back in. He had also seen the Dutchman, Horace Van Usschen.

'Your mother's testimony was indispensable,' Maigret replied. 'She's in La Roche-sur-Yon right now. I assume she'll be staying there for a few days. Maybe you'll go and see her?'

As he looked at the young man, he was thinking:

'Your hatred for your father, or the man who passes for your father, is only equalled by your irrational adoration for your mother.'

Then suddenly, without transition:

'The last time you spoke to her, she confirmed to you that Forlacroix wasn't your father, didn't she?'

'I already knew!' Albert muttered, staring at his boots.

'For quite a long time, I bet . . . Let's see! How old were you when you made that discovery? It must have been painful for you, wasn't it?'

'On the contrary!'

'Did you already hate Judge Forlacroix before you knew?'

'I certainly didn't love him!'

He was being cautious, weighing his words, like a peasant at the fair, and, whatever his feelings, he was avoiding flying off the handle, perhaps because he knew his own temper.

'How old were you when . . . ?'

'About sixteen. I was at high school in Luçon. I was taken out for several days. My father, I mean Forlacroix, had brought a famous doctor from Paris. I thought at first it was for my sister, but it was for me too.'

'Was your sister already . . . different?'

'She wasn't quite like anybody else.'

'And you?'

Albert gave a shudder and looked Maigret in the eyes. 'Nobody ever told me I was abnormal. At school I was an excellent pupil. The doctor examined me for hours, took samples, did tests. The judge stood over him all the time, anxious and overexcited, talking about things I didn't understand. Or rather, he talked about blood types, A, B. For several days, he waited impatiently for the test results, and when the paper arrived, with a letterhead from a laboratory in Paris, he looked at me coldly, with a kind of frozen smile, as if at last freed of a great weight . . .'

Albert was speaking slowly, still weighing his words.

'I questioned the older boys at school. I found out that a child always has the same blood type as its parents, and that in some countries this is admitted in court as evidence of paternity. Well, my blood wasn't the same type as my father's . . .'

He said this almost triumphantly.

'I thought of running away, but I didn't have any money. I'd have liked to join my mother, but I didn't have her address, and the judge clammed up whenever she was mentioned. I finished school. I did my military service. When I was discharged, I decided to live like the people around here . . .'

'Your temperament was more suited to strong physical activity, wasn't it? But tell me, why stay in the same village as the judge?'

'Because of my sister. I rented a house and started to

work at the mussel fields. I went to see the judge and asked him to give me my sister . . .'

'And of course he refused!'

'Why do you say "of course"?'

Again, there was suspicion in his eyes.

'Because the judge seems to love his daughter!'

'Or hate her!' Albert muttered between his teeth.

'Do you think so?'

'In any case, he hated me.'

He suddenly stood up.

'What does all this have to do with your case? You've been trying to make me talk, haven't you?'

He searched in his pocket but couldn't find a cigarette. Maigret held out the packet he had bought specially.

'Sit down, Forlacroix.'

'Has the judge confessed?'

'Confessed what?'

'You know perfectly well what I'm talking about.'

'He confessed to an old crime . . . He caught your mother with a man, back in Versailles, and killed the man . . .'

'Oh!'

'Tell me, Forlacroix . . .'

A silence. A heavy look from Maigret.

'Were you friends with Marcel Airaud?'

Silence again. As usual, the mayor had left some bottles of wine on the table, and Maigret now poured himself a glass.

'What difference does that make?'

'No difference. Not a big one, anyway. You're about the

same age. He's a mussel farmer, like you. You must have met at the mussel fields, at dances, whatever. I'm talking about the time when he wasn't yet climbing in through the window to see your sister.'

'We were friends, yes.'

'You live alone, don't you? It's quite unusual, at your age, such a liking for solitude. Your house is quite big.'

'A woman comes in every day to do the cleaning.'

'I know. And what about your meals? Don't tell me you do your own cooking?'

Sombre-eyed, Albert Forlacroix was wondering what Maigret was getting at.

'Sometimes. I'm not a big eater. A slice of ham, eggs. Some oysters before the meal. Occasionally I eat at the Hôtel du Port.'

'Strange . . .'

'What's strange?'

'Nothing! . . . You! . . . Basically, you live in L'Aiguillon the same way you'd live if you were in the middle of nowhere. Haven't you ever thought of getting married?'

'No.'

'And your friend Airaud?'

'He isn't my friend.'

'He isn't your friend any more, that's true . . . Did the two of you fall out when rumours started circulating that he sometimes spent the night with your sister?'

Now Forlacroix's unease was becoming visible. At first, despite his mistrust, he hadn't attached too much importance to Maigret's questions. Now it suddenly seemed to him as if a fine net was closing in around him. Where was the inspector going with all this? Maigret poured him a drink and pushed the packet of cigarettes in his direction.

'Drink. Smoke. Make yourself at home . . . We may be here for some time.'

Then Forlacroix swore to himself – and the thought could be read on his face:

'I won't say anything more! I won't answer any more of his questions!'

Maigret took a little walk around the room and stood for a while gazing at the bust of La République.

'Aren't you hungry?'

'No!'

'Maybe you've already had dinner? But I'm starving, and I wish I'd thought of bringing a few potatoes . . .'

Oh, yes! Oh, yes! That startled you, didn't it? Although, of course, you're a cool customer, we know that.

'Anyway, Airaud and you, built as you both are, are rather like the two village roosters. All the girls must be after you.'

'I'm not interested in girls.'

'But Airaud is! He even gets them pregnant sometimes! When you found out he was your sister's lover, you must have been indignant. I'm surprised there wasn't more damage.'

'We did fight . . .'

'Several times, I assume? Because he just carried on. It's quite puzzling. I don't know him very well. You know him much better than me. Do you think Marcel was genuinely in love with your sister?'

'I have no idea.'

'At any rate, that's what some people say. They say he intended to marry her and that he'd come to an agreement with the judge. If that had happened, you could have made it up between you, couldn't you? He'd have been your brother-in-law. It's a pity he ran away, because that doesn't exactly strengthen his case. You might as well know, I have a summons out for him. If he wasn't guilty, what reason could he have had to vanish like that and go to ground in the marshes?'

Cigarette followed cigarette. Every now and again, heavy footsteps could be heard on the path, people on their way to play cards at the Hôtel du Port.

And the 'singing session' went on. At times, Maigret turned to the wall, and an expression of discouragement crossed his face. There had been many others who had stood up to his questions for hours, sly, cunning, giving as good as they got.

The most famous of these interrogations, at Quai des Orfèvres, had lasted twenty-seven hours, and three officers had taken turns, not leaving the man a minute's respite.

But never before, perhaps, had he had such an inert mass to shift as Albert Forlacroix.

'Marcel's an only child, isn't he? And his mother's a widow, I think? Does she own any property? I ask that because, if he's found guilty, the life of that poor woman . . .'

'Don't worry about her. She's richer than most of the people in L'Aiguillon.'

'Good for her! Because the more I think about it . . . Look, do you want me to tell you, just between ourselves, how things happened? . . . One moment, I have to make

127

a phone call. I almost forgot, and that might have been serious . . . Hello, mademoiselle . . . It's me, yes . . . I owe you a lot of chocolates . . . No, that's true, you prefer marrons glacés . . . Anyway, my debt keeps getting bigger and bigger . . . The office is closed, I know . . . All the same, do you think you could get me Nantes? . . . The flying squad, yes . . . Thank you, mademoiselle . . .'

Come on! He mustn't slacken. He had to keep Forlacroix on tenterhooks.

'At first, he only wanted to have a bit of fun, which is quite understandable at his age. He didn't really care that your sister wasn't exactly like anyone else. Then he fell in love with her. He envisaged the possibility of marrying her. Didn't he talk to you about it at that point?'

'We didn't talk!'

'I forgot! Though since he went to see your father, he could have gone to see you, too, to tell you that it wasn't the way you thought, that his intentions were honourable. But if you tell me he didn't . . . Hello? . . . Yes! . . . Maigret here . . . Look, I'd like you to do me a favour . . . Do you have the address of Dr Janin's maid? . . . Good! Listen . . . It's a bit irregular . . . She must agree of her own free will, otherwise I'll have to wait until tomorrow to have her summoned by the examining magistrate . . . I'd like you to bring her here . . . Tonight, yes . . . It's no more than twenty kilometres . . . Where? . . . I'll probably be at the town hall . . . No, don't tell her anything! . . . Thank you!'

He hung up and assumed his most cordial air.

'I hope you didn't mind. A formality I'd forgotten . . . Suppose the gendarmes get their hands on Airaud . . .

They'll have to find him eventually, dammit! The marshes aren't a desert . . . Now this is what I think. Marcel envisages getting married. His mother probably dissuades him from marrying a girl who isn't quite normal. Even though he loves her, he's a bit worried himself . . .'

It was hot, of course, and the stove was purring. But was it the heat that caused beads of sweat to appear on Forlacroix's forehead?

'Then he remembers that a former shipmate of his, from the days when he was a sailor on the *Vengeur*, is now working as a doctor in Nantes. He goes to see him. He asks for his advice. Janin can't say anything without first seeing the girl. They both decide that he'll come here and examine her . . .'

Albert stubbed out his cigarette beneath his heel and lit another.

'You must admit it holds together, psychologically speaking. I don't know your former friend Airaud as well as you do. Before anything else, he's a peasant. That means he's cautious by nature. He wants to get married, but all the same he'd like to make sure his future wife isn't completely mad . . . What do you think?'

'I don't know!' Albert said curtly.

'Have your drink. Are you sure you're not hungry? . . . In my opinion . . . and I may be mistaken . . . in my opinion, Marcel doesn't dare tell your father. To be blunt about it, your father is giving him his daughter, but giving her as she is. Plus, if she was healthy and normal, it's unlikely he'd marry her off to a mussel farmer . . .'

And here Maigret turned vulgar, laughing heartily like a travelling salesman telling crude stories.

'You can just see our Airaud telling his future father-in-law: "All right! You're very kind. I'll take your daughter, but I'd like an expert opinion first . . ."'

A look from Albert, a look full of hatred. Maigret pretended not to see it.

'So he has to have the girl examined without the judge knowing. Which is why I think he chose a Tuesday. That evening, Forlacroix is shut up for hours in the library on the ground floor with his friends. They're talking loudly. Drinking. Laughing. Nobody will have any inkling of what's going on upstairs . . . There's only one thing that bothers me, Albert . . . Do you mind if I call you that? . . . Yes, one detail bothers me. I know Janin is a bit unorthodox, even something of a hothead. All the same, there are rules the medical profession tends to follow to the letter . . .

'Just see how events pan out and then tell me if there isn't something not quite right . . .'

He, too, was hot and he mopped his brow and filled his pipe. At times like these, he realized what an effort a variety performer, for example, had to make to carry his audience with him, to keep a crowd of people in suspense for minutes on end, come what may . . .

He had only one man in front of him. But what a bad audience! The kind that declares in advance: 'This is stupid! I won't go along with it!'

'Listen, my dear Forlacroix. Janin gets off the bus. Airaud must have arranged to meet him outside, not far from the Hôtel du Port. He doesn't want anybody to know about this visit.

'Why does Janin feel the need to go into the hotel and order his dinner for that evening?

'Whatever the reason, he comes out. He meets Marcel. It isn't quite time to go to the Forlacroix house. The judge's guests haven't arrived yet. There's no way to see the girl on her own before nine in the evening.

'What do you think the two men could have done all that time? It was raining. I can't see them walking in the dark for hours on end. It's also curious that nobody in L'Aiguillon ran into them . . .

'Plus, they had something to eat! At least, we have evidence that Janin did . . . I don't mind telling you this, even though it's meant to be confidential . . . When they did the post mortem, they found the remains of a fairly copious meal in his stomach.

'Where could they have gone to eat, do you think?'

And Maigret, who had been walking, stopped for a moment and gave Forlacroix a firm slap on the shoulder.

'That's not all, my friend! The guests have arrived. Brénéol and his wife and daughter, followed by the Marsacs. Now's the time. They still have to get up to your sister Lise's bedroom, which is on the first floor. Marcel is in the habit of climbing along the wall . . .

'What I wonder is whether Doctor Janin, however unorthodox he may have been, also proceeded to clamber up the front of the house.

'It's the only possible hypothesis.

'Is Airaud with him?

'Whatever the case, it's quite possible the drama had taken place by midnight. You gave us the proof of that.'

'I did?'

'Oh, yes! Have you forgotten your own statements? Statements the judge has confirmed in detail . . . When he came up to the first floor after his guests had left, in other words around midnight, he found you sitting at the top of the stairs.'

Silence. Another pipe. More coal in the stove.

'By the way, if you'd fallen out with the judge, why did you keep a key to the house?'

'To see my sister.'

'Did you see her that night?'

'No!'

'And you didn't hear any noise, did you, either in the room or in the fruitery, even though you were sitting almost directly in front of the door? That's what makes me think it was all over by then . . .'

He gulped down a whole glass of wine and wiped his lips.

'That would seem to put Judge Forlacroix in the clear, but not a bit of it . . . How long were you in the house before the guests left? Not long, I suppose, since you knew the time they usually left?'

'Five or ten minutes.'

'Five or ten minutes . . . They were playing bridge . . . In bridge, there's always a dummy. In the course of the evening, Forlacroix may have taken advantage of the fact that he was a dummy to pop upstairs and make sure everything was all right. He sees a man he doesn't know. There's a hammer within arm's reach. He strikes him . . .'

'What are you getting at?' Albert Forlacroix asked.

'Nothing. We're just chatting. I've been wanting to talk to you about all these things for a long time now. One question occurs to me. Did Marcel Airaud enter the house at the same time as the doctor?'

'Why do you ask me?'

'No, obviously, you couldn't know, could you? He might have come in with him and been present at the examination. He could also simply have announced the visitor to your sister Lise, who was fairly reasonable when she wasn't having one of her attacks . . . You see, my friend, all hypotheses are allowed . . .

'If Airaud did go in, it's possible he quarrelled with Janin . . . If Janin tells him, for example: "You can't marry this girl . . ."'

'He loves her! He asked the man for advice. But who knows if, when all is revealed to him . . .

'Last but not least, your sister herself could have . . .'

'You think my sister would have been capable . . .'

'Calm down! Like I said, we're just chatting! We're considering all the possibilities. Janin examines her, asks her the kind of specific, even indiscreet, questions a doctor feels permitted to ask . . .

'She has an attack . . . Or she is just afraid he'll stop Marcel from marrying her . . .'

Phew! His cheeks were red, and his eyes shining.

'That's why it would be interesting to know if Airaud was in the house or waiting outside . . . It's obvious that his running away doesn't make him look good. People don't usually hide if they have nothing to feel guilty about. Unless . . .'

He seemed to think this over carefully and then once again slapped Albert on the shoulder.

'Oh, yes! He does have an answer for us when we arrest him . . . Let's say he stayed outside. He waits. He doesn't see his friend come back. Late that night, he climbs the wall, gets into the fruitery and discovers the doctor's body. He tells himself it was Lise who killed him.

'The investigation begins. He's afraid they'll suspect her. He loves her. So to divert suspicion from his fiancée, he pretends to run away.

'Is it a way of gaining time, of maybe getting the case dropped? What do you think?'

'I don't think anything!'

'Obviously, you haven't the slightest idea where Airaud is hiding. Don't answer yet. You were his friend. He was going to become your brother-in-law. It's perfectly understandable that you wouldn't want to give him up to the law . . . I say it's perfectly understandable, on a human level, that is, but not from the legal point of view. Do you get my meaning? . . . Let's suppose you've seen Airaud since he ran away and didn't say anything. It's only a supposition. He may still be wandering around the countryside. It'd be hard not to draw certain conclusions.'

'What conclusions?' Albert asked in a slow voice, uncrossing his legs and crossing them in the other direction, letting the ash from his cigarette fall on his jacket.

'It may be thought, for example, that you, too, want to save your sister . . . You were on the landing for five or ten minutes, but we have no proof of that . . . You didn't set foot in the hotel that evening, did you?'

'Not after nine o'clock.'

'You must have had a key to your sister's room. You admitted as much yourself when you said you'd kept a key to the front door so that you could visit her. That key would have been useless if, once inside . . . But I guess you lost that second key, because on a particular night I saw you knock the door in with your shoulder . . . Maybe you were just in an emotional state, or were you trying to pull the wool over our eyes?'

Silence. Albert was staring pensively at the dusty floor. By the time he raised his eyes, he had made his mind up.

'Is this an interrogation?'

'It's whatever you want it to be.'

'And am I obliged to answer?'

'No!'

'In that case, I have nothing to say.'

And he stubbed out his cigarette with his boot.

Maigret walked around the room two or three more times, made sure there was no more wine in the bottle, and turned the crank of the telephone.

'Oh, good, you aren't in bed yet, mademoiselle. Could you put me through to the Hôtel du Port? Thank you! . . . Hello? Is that you Thérèse? . . . Call Inspector Méjat for me, my dear . . . Méjat? . . . Look, old chap, can you go to Albert Forlacroix's house? . . . Go across the back yard . . . At the end of it, you'll find a kind of shed . . . A man is in there, sleeping on a straw mattress . . . No, I don't think he's dangerous! . . . Be careful all the same . . . Yes, put the

handcuffs on him, it's safer . . . And bring him to me . . .
That's right . . . Forlacroix? . . . No, he won't protest . . .
He's here. He's agreed to it.'

Maigret hung up with a smile.

'Inspector Méjat was afraid you'd lodge a complaint for
forcible entry. Strictly speaking, it's not allowed without a
warrant, especially in the middle of the night . . . Cigarette? . . . Really? . . . If I'd been there myself, I don't think
I'd have resisted the temptation to take down one of those
succulent sausages hanging above the fireplace.'

Then, in a softer voice:

'When exactly did you slaughter the pig?'

10. *Didine's Little Dishes*

During the minutes that followed, Maigret seemed to have forgotten his companion; he began by taking his watch from his pocket; he slowly rewound it, with exaggerated care, took it off its chain and put it down on the table as if, from now on, the passage of time was going to be important.

Then he waited. Albert Forlacroix didn't move, didn't even heave a sigh. He must have been ill at ease on his rickety chair. He must have wanted to shift, maybe to scratch his cheek, or his nose, to cross and uncross his legs. But, precisely because Maigret was keeping quite still, he forced himself with grim determination to do the same.

From where he was, he couldn't see Maigret's face as he pretended to be absorbed in staring at the stove. Otherwise, he would no doubt have caught a slight, almost playful smile.

It was just a professional ploy, of course, the kind of little trick designed to disconcert a man!

Footsteps outside. Maigret walked calmly to the door and opened it. Marcel Airaud was there in front of him, with handcuffs on his wrists, and Inspector Méjat, swollen with his own importance, was holding on to the handcuffs. A gendarme was behind them in the shadows.

Marcel didn't seem upset and only blinked because he

was startled by the light. He stood there while Forlacroix remained on his chair.

'Can you take that one next door?' Maigret said to the inspector, pointing to Albert.

Next door was the ballroom, with its white walls, its paper chains hanging from the ceiling, its benches all around for the mothers. Between the two rooms, a glass door.

'Sit down, Airaud. I'll be with you in a moment.'

But Marcel preferred to remain standing. Maigret gave his instructions, posted the gendarme to keep an eye on Forlacroix and sent Méjat off to fetch sandwiches and bottles of beer.

It was all happening as if in slow motion. Forlacroix and Airaud must be observing Maigret's behaviour with astonishment. And yet they had been caught up in the mechanism for some time now.

Was Marcel Airaud capable of humour? It was quite possible. He didn't seem thrown in any way by Maigret's overwhelming composure. He watched him as he came and went and simply stood there with a vague smile hovering over his lips.

On the other side of the glass door, Forlacroix had sat down on the bench, his back to the wall, his legs stretched out, and the gendarme, who was taking his role seriously, had sat down facing him with his eyes fixed on him.

'Have you been hiding at your friend Albert's house for a long time?' Maigret suddenly asked, looking elsewhere.

As soon as he heard his own voice, he had the feeling it

was pointless. He waited a moment, then turned to his prisoner.

'Am I under arrest?' Marcel asked, glancing at his handcuffs.

'I have here a warrant signed by the examining magistrate.'

'In that case, I'll only answer the magistrate, and in the presence of my lawyer.'

Maigret looked him up and down, without surprise.

'Come in!' he cried to Méjat, who had knocked.

Méjat came in, his arms laden with little packets, and placed everything on the table: pâté, ham, bread, bottles of beer. He tried to whisper in Maigret's ear.

'Speak up!' Maigret grunted.

'I said, Thérèse is in the courtyard. She seems to suspect something. She immediately asked me if he had been arrested.'

Maigret shrugged, made himself a sandwich, poured himself a drink and again looked Marcel Airaud up and down. There was no point in insisting, he was sure.

'Take him next door, Méjat. Tell the gendarme to stop them talking to each other. As for you, come back here.'

He walked. He ate. He muttered to himself. He shrugged. Every time he passed the door, he could see them on the bench, there in the big white room, the gendarme watching them with knitted brows.

'Is everything all right, chief?' Méjat asked, coming back into the room.

He fell silent, because one look from the inspector had sufficed. He wasn't yet used to it. He didn't know how to act. And Maigret was still eating, stuffing over-large pieces in his mouth and, still chewing, going over to the door and gazing in at his two captured animals through the glass.

Suddenly, he turned.

'Go and fetch Didine.'

'There's no need to go far. When I came in, she was standing guard just ten metres from here.'

'Bring her in.'

'What about Thérèse?'

'Did I mention Thérèse?'

Soon afterwards, Didine came into the ballroom and stopped in front of the two men with a satisfied look on her face, especially pleased to see the shiny handcuffs on Marcel Airaud's wrists.

'Come in, Didine. I need you.'

'So you got him after all!'

'Sit down, Didine. I won't offer you a beer . . . Or should I?'

'I don't like it . . . So you arrested him in the end.'

'Listen to me, Didine. Take your time answering. This is very important . . . You, Méjat, either sit down or go for a walk, but don't just stand there looking at me like an idiot . . . Now then, my good lady. Let's suppose that one afternoon, you're suddenly told that someone is coming to have dinner at your house. Someone from the town. What would you do?'

She might have been expected to react with surprise at the unexpectedness of the question, but that would have been not to know Didine well. Her features became sharper as she considered the question. It was pointless to advise her to think it over carefully. She was taking her time.

'What kind of person?' she asked.

'A respectable person.'

'And I'd only be told about it in the afternoon? At what time?'

'Let's say four thirty or five.'

The three men on the other side of the glass, Airaud, Forlacroix and the gendarme, were looking into the room, but they were in the position that Maigret had been in that afternoon: they could see lips moving but heard only a vague murmur.

'I don't know if you've quite understood me. You know what's available in L'Aiguillon, the local habits. You know what can be found at any hour when it comes to food and drink.'

'It'd be too late to kill a chicken,' she said as if to herself. 'It wouldn't be tender. Not to mention that it'd take too long to pluck and gut . . . What day of the week are you talking about, inspector?'

Méjat was stunned. As for Maigret, he wasn't smiling at all.

'A Tuesday.'

'I'm starting to understand. It's that Tuesday you mean, isn't it? It's as if it was meant to be. I said to my husband . . . That man, I said to him, must have eaten somewhere. He certainly didn't eat at the restaurant. He didn't eat at the judge's house either.'

'Answer my question, Didine. What would you have served him on a Tuesday?'

'Not meat. They do the slaughtering on a Monday here. On Tuesday, the meat's too fresh. It would have been tough ... Wait! How was the tide that Tuesday? High tide was about eight in the evening, wasn't it? That means Polyte was at home. In that case, I'd have gone to Polyte's. He always goes out trawling with the morning tide. So he must have come back at about midday. If he had a good piece ...'

'Where does Polyte live?'

'You won't find him at home. He's in the café. Not at the Hôtel du Port, the one opposite ...'

'Do you hear that, Méjat?'

Méjat went out without needing to be asked twice.

'When Polyte has a nice pair of soles, or a nice dory ...' Didine continued. 'That's the beginnings of a decent meal. As long as there's ham in the house. But ... Wait, inspector! ... There isn't only Polyte ... It depends whether or not you like lapwings. Because then, it's worth going to see old Rouillon, who goes out hunting every morning.'

The three men were still there, beyond the glass. Forlacroix's gaze was sombre. Marcel Airaud, despite his handcuffs, was smoking a cigarette and squinting because of the smoke.

'Only, to prepare lapwings, you need ...'

Méjat crossed the ballroom in the company of a thin fisherman with a pointed nose and a brick-red complexion, who stopped in surprise in front of Marcel.

'You here? D'you give yourself up?'

'Come in!' Maigret called. 'Are you the one they call Polyte?'

He peered anxiously at Didine. What could she have told them about him for them to call him in?

'Now then, Polyte. You remember last Tuesday . . .'

'Tuesday . . .' he repeated, like a man who wasn't quite all there.

'The day of the fair at Saint-Michel!' Didine said. 'The day when the tide was 108 . . .'

'Let's see . . . What was I doing that day?'

'Getting drunk like every other day!' Didine said, again feeling the need to butt in.

'Where were you during the afternoon?'

And Didine once more, tirelessly:

'In the bistro, of course! If he could, he'd sleep there. Isn't that right, Polyte?'

'What I'd like to know is if anyone came to see you that afternoon and asked you for a nice piece of fish.'

Forlacroix's sombre gaze, in the other room. Polyte thought it over, turning to Didine as if to ask her for advice.

'The day when the tide was 108 . . . Don't you remember?' he asked, with disarming candour.

And suddenly he turned towards the glass door and slapped his own forehead, while a triumphant smile lit up Didine's face.

'It's Albert who came,' he declared. 'I remember, because he was in a great hurry. I was playing cards with Deveaud and Fraigne. Wait just a minute, I told him. Then, as he was getting impatient, I told him to go and get some soles from my boat.'

'How many?'

'I don't know how many he took. I told him to help himself. We still haven't settled up . . .'

'That's all I wanted to know. You can go. By the way, Didine, where does Albert Forlacroix's housekeeper live?'

'Actually, she's his daughter.'

'Polyte's?'

'Yes. But she doesn't live with her father. If you want to see her, you'd better hurry, because she goes to bed early. Especially as, just for a change, she's expecting. One every year! Some girls are anybody's.'

'Méjat! Can you go and fetch her? And don't upset her, eh?'

He was starting to get excited. In the doorway, Polyte was still waiting for permission to go. At last he walked off with Méjat, pointing him in the direction of his daughter's house.

'God knows how come the men aren't disgusted by her. You'll see her. Maybe she'll clean herself up before she comes! If I had to eat what she's touched . . .'

She was surprised to see Maigret standing motionless in the middle of the room, listening to nothing, looking at nothing. An idea had just struck him. Suddenly, he rushed to the telephone.

'I hope you weren't in bed, mademoiselle? Get me the Albert-Premier nursing home in La Roche-sur-Yon . . . Number 41 . . . Ring until someone answers . . . There's at least one nurse on duty . . . Yes, I'm very grateful . . .'

He had forgotten Didine, who now asked calmly:

'Do you think it's Marcel? If you want my advice, knowing both of them . . .'

'Be quiet!' he cried, like a man in a temper.

He couldn't take his eyes off the telephone. For hours, for days now, he'd been searching . . .

'Hello? . . . . The Albert-Premier? . . . Who am I speaking to? . . . Tell me, mademoiselle, is the doctor still there? . . . What's that, he's at home? . . . Can you put me through to his apartment? . . .'

His cheeks were flushed and he was biting the stem of his pipe, looking mechanically at Didine as if he didn't recognize her.

'Hello? . . . Is that you, doctor? . . . You were just eating? . . . I'm so sorry . . . Detective Chief Inspector Maigret, yes . . . I wanted to ask you . . . Of course, you've examined her . . . What? . . . More serious than we thought? . . . That's not what I called you about . . . I'd like to ask you if you discovered anything unexpected . . . Yes . . . What? . . . What's that you say? . . . Are you certain? . . . Three months? . . . Thank you, doctor . . . Yes, of course, you'll make an official report . . . Has she calmed down? . . . Thank you . . . Once again, I'm sorry to have disturbed you . . .'

He was on edge. When he discovered the old woman still sitting there on her chair, he said:

'Now run along, my dear Didine. You've been very kind, but I don't need you any more for the moment.'

She stood up reluctantly, but didn't go yet.

'I bet I can guess what he told you . . .'

'Good for you. Now just run along! Wait next door if you want, but . . .'

'She's pregnant, isn't she?'

He couldn't believe his ears. He was almost starting to be afraid of her!

'I don't have time to answer you. Just go! And above all, keep your mouth shut . . .'

He opened the door. He was about to close it again when Méjat arrived, accompanied by a girl with dirty hair falling down the back of her neck.

'She didn't want to come with me because she was about to go to bed . . .'

At that moment, a little event occurred. At the sight of his maid, Forlacroix had stood up, as if wanting to intervene. The gendarme no doubt made a mistake in touching his arm, which had the effect of restoring his composure, and he sat down again.

'Good! Come in for a moment. I only have a couple of questions to ask you. What time do you finish work at Albert Forlacroix's house?'

'Sometimes at three, sometimes at four.'

'Don't you make his dinner?'

'I never make any of his meals. He does all his own cooking. He likes it!'

She said these last words with what might have been irony or contempt.

'I assume you do the washing up?'

'Yes, I get the dirty work. And there's plenty of that in the house! Men, when you see them outside, are all spruced up. But when you have to clean up after them . . .'

'How often does he have guests?'

'Who?'

'Your employer.'

'Never! Who'd he have as a guest?'

'Don't you ever find several dirty plates in the morning?'

'It happened last week.'

'Wednesday morning, wasn't it?'

'It might have been Wednesday . . . And ashes every-where. They'd been smoking cigars.'

'Do you know who his visitor was?'

She turned towards the glass door and replied guile-lessly, holding her belly in both hands with a mechanical gesture:

'Why don't you ask him?'

'Thank you for your help. You can go to bed now.'

'Is he the one who did it?'

It didn't surprise her. It didn't scare her. It wasn't much more than curiosity on her part. Sure enough, she added:

'I'm only asking so as to know if I need to go there tomorrow . . .'

Voices could be heard out in the street, beyond the gates of the town hall. People had had wind of something. A little group had formed. They stood looking at the cream curtains, behind which they could sometimes see shadows passing, especially the thick silhouette of Maigret, whose pipe occasionally, when he was at a certain angle, appeared immense, almost as large as his head.

'I think they've arrested both of them!' Polyte's daughter announced when she had been allowed to leave and the onlookers questioned her.

She was so sleepy that she didn't linger, and the noise of her clogs could be heard as she walked away over the frost-hardened cobbles. The door opened. It was Méjat, trying to recognize the faces in the darkness.

'Is Thérèse still there?' he asked.

From a shadowy area over to the side, a form emerged. 'What do you want with me?'

'Come inside! The inspector wants to talk to you.'

As she passed Marcel, she looked him in the eyes, but didn't open her mouth.

'Come in, Thérèse. Don't be afraid. I'd like to ask you a simple question . . . Did you know that Lise Forlacroix was pregnant?'

Hearing this, she turned towards the glass door, and it looked as if she might rush at Airaud, who couldn't have had any idea what was going on.

'It isn't true!' she said, thinking better of it. 'You're trying to trick me.'

'I assure you, Thérèse, Lise Forlacroix is three months' pregnant . . .'

'That's why!' she said in a low voice, as if to herself.

'That's why what?'

'He wanted to marry her.'

'So you admit he wanted to marry her? But he didn't tell you the reason? Well, now you know the reason. You know that . . .'

'What about me, don't I have a child? Aren't I just as good as the judge's daughter? Did he marry me?'

It must have been strange to watch her through the glass, because it was obvious she was angry, but hard to guess why.

'You know, even that night . . .'

'Yes, what did you say to him that night?'

'I told him that if he married her, I'd be at the church with his son and that I'd make a scene . . .'

'Hold on a moment . . . You spoke to him on Tuesday night? Where?'

She hesitated for a moment, then shrugged. 'In the street . . .'

'What time was it?'

'Maybe just before midnight.'

'Whereabouts in the street?'

She turned again with a vicious look towards the glass. 'All right, I'll tell you . . . Too bad! . . . At about ten, just as I was going to bed, I saw a light in Lise's window . . .'

'The window of her bedroom or the window of the fruitery?'

'Her bedroom.'

'Are you sure you didn't mix them up?'

She gave an ironic laugh. 'Of course I'm sure! I've spied on the two of them often enough! I tried to sleep but I couldn't. I got up again and decided to go and wait for him outside.'

'Intending to do what?'

'The usual thing,' she admitted wearily.

'You didn't threaten him with anything else except making a scene in church?'

'I told him I'd kill myself in his house . . .'

'Would you have done it?'

'I have no idea. I crept outside. It was raining. I'd even put my coat over my head. I wondered if he'd be staying late. Maybe, if he'd stayed too long, I'd have decided to climb up.'

'And what happened?'

'I was walking along, talking to myself, as I often do. I wasn't looking in front of me, because there was nobody in the streets . . . Suddenly, I bumped into someone. It was him. I was so surprised that I cried out.'

'Where was he?'

'Near the wall, behind the judge's house.'

'What was he doing? Coming out?'

'No! He wasn't doing anything. He seemed to be waiting. I asked him what he was waiting for.'

'What did he reply?'

'Nothing! He twisted my wrists. He was furious. "If I catch you spying on me again," he growled, "I don't know what I'll do . . ."'

'What time was it?'

'Not far off midnight, as I said . . . Maybe a little later . . .'

'Was there still a light on in the bedroom?'

'I don't know. You can't see it from there, because of the wall. "Go to bed, you bitch!" he yelled at me. "Do you understand? And if ever . . ." I'd never seen him so angry with me.'

Another glance at the other side of the glass. There, in the ballroom, Airaud was as calm as ever. The gendarme must have given him another cigarette, which he was holding askew because of the handcuffs.

'Do you mind waiting next door, Thérèse? I may need you again.'

When the door had closed again, a voice – Méjat's – said:

'Well, well, chief. I think . . .'

'You think what?'

'I think that . . . that . . .'

Poor man! He had tried to be nice, to congratulate Maigret on the results obtained. But the only response was a glare.

'Well? What do you think? Answer me. You're going to find the evidence, are you? Go and fetch me some beer! . . . Or rather, no . . . Bring me some real hooch . . . Calvados, rum, whatever . . . What time is it?'

It was midnight, and there was nobody left outside but three onlookers who stood there stamping their feet, hoping to finally hear something.

11. *The Doctor's Maid*

The hum of an engine, the noise of brakes, the slamming of car doors. A moment later, two inspectors entered the ballroom in the company of a woman in her thirties, who looked dazed.

'Sorry, sir. We had a flat tyre on the way here. The jack wouldn't work. We . . .'

'Is this her?' Maigret asked, examining the young woman, who was quite lost, her eyes darting all over in such a way that she saw nothing.

'She didn't want to come, because of her sister-in-law who's ill. We had to promise to take her back tonight.'

Suddenly, the woman noticed the handcuffs and gave a muffled cry.

'Do you recognize him?' Maigret asked. 'Take a good look at him. Tell me if he recently paid your employer a visit.'

'I recognize them,' she replied, recovering her composure.

'You . . . what did you say? . . . You recognize *them*?'

'Well, yes! I recognize both of them, because they came together.'

'And they both saw the doctor in his office?'

'Both of them. Not immediately, because the doctor wasn't there. I advised them to come back the following day, but they preferred to sit in the waiting room for more than two hours.'

'That's it!' Maigret muttered. 'I don't need you any more.'

'Shall we take her back?' the two inspectors asked, somewhat annoyed.

'If you like . . . Wait . . . Here's Méjat bringing something to drink . . . Only, I don't know if there are enough glasses.'

Then Didine again rose and touched the inspector's arm.

'In the cupboard,' she whispered.

'What's in the cupboard?'

'Glasses. There are always some, for council meetings. Would you like me to wipe them?'

She knew everything! She had seen and heard everything!

The policemen drank. As the doctor's maid was feeling cold, she, too, was given a little alcohol, but it only made her cough desperately.

The blood had gone to Maigret's head. He seemed so tense that Méjat was watching him with a certain anxiety. Suddenly, he opened the door. The inspectors had left. The car was setting off again.

'Come here, you!' he called to Airaud with unexpected abruptness. 'Take off his handcuffs, Méjat. He looks stupid like that. Come in! Close the door, Méjat. And you, I advise you not to try and be clever, do you understand? I've had just about enough! That's right, I've had enough.'

It was so unexpected that Marcel lost his composure.

'I bet you think you're intelligent. You're pleased with yourself, aren't you? Oh, yes! . . . Look at yourself in the mirror. And please, don't keep shifting from one leg to the other like a bear . . . What did your father do?'

It was so surprising that, despite his determination not to answer, Airaud could not help murmuring:

'He was a mussel farmer.'

'And you're a mussel farmer! And you imagine that a judge's daughter is something extraordinary, don't you? And you don't realize that you're nothing but a young fool that people laugh at. How long ago was it that Forlacroix made it up with you?'

A hostile silence.

'All right, don't answer. That makes you look even better!'

This time, getting carried away, Maigret spoke so loudly that it was impossible for those on the other side of the door not to hear, if not all the words, at least enough to catch the drift of what he was saying.

Talking all the while, walking about, chewing the stem of his pipe, he poured himself a drink with such frenzy that Méjat was astounded.

'That's it, don't answer! You're too stupid anyway and wouldn't have much to say . . . Wasn't your affair with Thérèse enough for you? Because you almost married her, didn't you? Everybody knows that. Only, everybody also knew what you didn't know.'

'I did know . . .'

'What?'

'That she was seeing other men.'

'OK! And you didn't marry her. That's something at least. You realized you were being taken for a ride. Only, Thérèse is nothing but a hotel maid, the daughter of a woman who sells fish in the street. Whereas the other girl . . .'

Marcel's features had hardened, and Maigret, in spite of his apparent excitement, glanced at his big fists, which were clenched. Didn't he turn away for a moment to wipe away a smile that rose to his lips? Didn't he need to take a big swig of his drink in order to keep up the tone?

'Monsieur was quite proud of being the lover of a Forlacroix girl, the daughter of a judge, someone who played the piano . . .'

'Listen, inspector . . .'

'Shut up! You won't speak until there's a lawyer present. You told me that. Monsieur is in love. Monsieur is raring to go. And when old Forlacroix, who's been watching him from behind his door, lets him in, Monsieur is reduced to a stammering little boy . . .'

'"What! You love my daughter? That's no problem! She's yours! Take her. Marry her."'

'That's it, isn't it? And this big lump who's strong enough to kill an ox can't see further than the end of his nose.

'"Yes, sir, I'll marry her! Yes, sir, I'm an honest man and my intentions are honourable . . ."'

'He's so moved, so filled with happiness and pride that he can't hold it in and goes to see his enemy, young Forlacroix, who's vowed a hundred times to smash his face in.

'"You have the wrong idea about me. I want to marry your sister. Let's make it up between us."'

On the other side of the glass, Forlacroix was craning his neck, trying to hear, and old Didine had moved to the very end of the bench.

'Well, my boy, there's something I can tell you for sure, which is that they both tricked you. You still don't understand, do you? You told yourself they'd recognized your merits and were opening their arms to you.

'Only your good old mother suspected something. And I'm sure you were angry with her when she advised you to be cautious, not to get carried away.

'"I assure you, Mother, Lise isn't as mad as people think. When she's happy and well looked after . . ."

'The same old story! You poor fool!'

Marcel was breathing heavily now. Maigret looked him up and down and winked at Méjat, who wasn't quite sure what that meant.

'I'm sure it was your mother who had the one little spark of common sense. What could the poor woman do to persuade a boy as stubborn and excitable as you?

'"At least have her examined by a doctor. What if she's completely mad?"

'That's when you think of your old shipmate Janin. You convince Albert that you only want what's best. If, after examining Lise, Janin decides that . . .

'What? That's not the way it happened? Don't answer! You're not saying anything without a lawyer present, isn't that right?

'Of course, Albert knows that his sister's pregnant . . .'

It was so sudden that Maigret didn't have time to move back. Or maybe this was the reaction he was after. Marcel had grabbed him by his lapel and was about to shake him.

'What did you say? . . . What did you say? . . .'

'Do you want the doctor at the clinic to confirm it to you? Later. You just have to talk to him on the phone.'

'Lise is . . .'

'Pregnant. Oh, yes! It does happen! That's why the judge is suddenly so happy to let his daughter marry a big brute like you.

'And that's why Albert goes with you to Nantes. He doesn't trust you. He doesn't want his sister and himself to become the laughing stock of L'Aiguillon.

'There was one thing that bothered me. I wondered if Janin had really agreed to climb along the wall to go and see a patient.

'Of course not! There was no need! You can't have him come to your house because then your mother would know, and you prefer to keep her out of this.

'The three of you have dinner at Albert's house. I can even tell you that you ate sole.

'Then, when the guests have arrived at the judge's house, when the game of bridge has started and the way is clear, it's Albert who takes the doctor there. He has the key. It isn't difficult to get up to the first floor without making any noise . . . I became suspicious when he saw fit, in front of me, to knock the door in with his shoulder. If he had a key to the front door, it was more than likely . . . But that's no concern of yours . . . He lets Doctor Janin into his sister's room. He waits . . .

'And you're left pacing up and down outside, near the wall you're so used to climbing . . .'

Maigret turned to the door and saw Albert Forlacroix standing beyond it, looking menacing.

'You had a strange time waiting there, didn't you? Thérèse interfering and threatening you . . . You wonder why the two men haven't come down again . . . Well, I'm going to tell you. After examining the girl, Dr Janin joined Albert in the fruitery. What he told him isn't hard to guess. The first thing he must have said was: "Your sister is expecting a baby."

'Then . . . Look at him . . . No, not the inspector . . . Turn to the door . . . Look at his face . . .'

Albert Forlacroix stood there, pale-faced, and you could see a strange dampness on his lips and a pinching of his nostrils.

'Come in, Forlacroix. You'll be able to hear better. I'm going to tell you what the doctor told you. He told you that your sister was incurable, that it would be dishonest to throw her into the arms of an honest man, that her place was in a clinic, and that his duty as a doctor was to . . .'

'It isn't true!' Albert uttered in a toneless voice.

'What isn't true?'

'I didn't kill him. It was my sister . . .'

He bent his head forward as if about to charge.

'That's the story you told Marcel when you came back down on your own. Unfortunately, if Lise had killed the doctor with a hammer from the fruitery, it would never have occurred to her to then wipe the handle. Has she ever even heard of fingerprints? No, my friend! The one who struck him was you, in a fit of anger, and you're going to have another one if you're not careful . . .

'The doctor told you that he wanted to tell his friend Airaud the truth.

'You insisted. You wanted the marriage to go ahead, come what may.

'Then you had one of your usual tempers.

'And do you know . . . Yes, I'd swear to it . . . Do you know what must have gone through Dr Janin's mind when he saw you coming at him like a maniac?

'He must have thought your sister wasn't the only mad one in the family and that . . .'

Albert Forlacroix charged, his features twisted, his eyes shining, his breathing hoarse. But before he could reach Maigret, Marcel had grabbed him by the shoulders, and both of them were rolling on the floor.

Unconcerned by what was happening, Maigret went to the table, poured himself a drink, relit his pipe and wiped his forehead.

'Put the handcuffs on him if you can, Méjat. It's safer.'

It wasn't an easy task, because the two fighters were of more or less equal strength. Forlacroix had managed to seize his opponent's thumb between his teeth and was biting savagely. Marcel was unable to hold back a scream. A handcuff clicked. Méjat couldn't get hold of the other hand and so, in a panic, he started clumsily hitting out like a deaf man, pounding his fists on Albert's face.

Didine's face was pressed to the glass, her nose spread,

a gleam in her eyes, the beginnings of a smile of content-
ment on her thin lips.

'Well?'

'There, chief . . . That's it . . .'

The other wrist had at last been imprisoned in the steel
ring.

Marcel Airaud got unsteadily to his feet, squeezing his
bloodstained left thumb with his right hand. He, too,
seized the bottle of alcohol from the table. But it wasn't
to drink from it. It was to pour some on his wound. The
bone was exposed.

The gendarme knocked at the door and half opened it.

'Do you need me?'

At that moment Maigret looked at all of them, one
after the other, with a vacant eye. He looked at Didine,
who was nodding smugly, Méjat with blood on his hands
and an expression of disgust on his face, the startled gendarme, Airaud wrapping a check handkerchief around
his thumb . . .

Albert Forlacroix got up painfully, or rather sat up on
the floor, and remained there, dazed, his body still shaken
with spasms.

The silence was such that you could hear distinctly the
ticking of the watch on the table. Maigret put it back on
the end of its chain. It showed ten minutes past two.

'He made me believe it was her,' Airaud murmured,
looking stupidly at his thumb. 'To divert suspicion . . .'

'Will you take care of them, Méjat?'

He went out, lit his pipe and walked slowly to the harbour. He could hear scurrying footsteps behind him. The

sea was becoming swollen. The beams of the lighthouses joined in the sky. The moon had just risen, and the judge's house emerged from the darkness, all white, a crude, livid, unreal white.

The footsteps had stopped. Two figures had come together on the corner of the street. Didine had rejoined her one-eyed customs officer, who had been waiting for her, and was talking to him in a low voice.

'I wonder if they'll cut his head off!' she said, pulling her shawl tight about her shoulders to keep warm.

Soon afterwards, a door creaked. They had returned home. They were going to climb up into the high bed with its feather eiderdown and would probably whisper in the darkness for quite some time to come.

Left alone, Maigret caught himself murmuring dreamily: 'And that's it!'

It was over. He might never return to L'Aiguillon. From now on, it would be like one of those distant land-scapes, tiny but meticulously accurate, that you see in glass globes: a little world . . . People from far and wide . . . The judge sitting by the fire . . . Lise in her bed, her full lips, her gold-speckled pupils, her swollen breast . . . Constantinesco in the apartment in Versailles, and his daughter on her way to the Conservatoire . . . Old Horace Van Usschen in his excessively light trousers and white woollen cap . . . Thérèse who would get someone to marry her, come what may . . . The widow Airaud, who had been thinking she would be alone for ever in her house, and who would suddenly be reunited with her giant of a son . . .

A regular sound, coming from out of the darkness, made him jump. He remembered that it was old Bariteau, off to lay his eel nets.

Come to think of it, how high was the tide tonight?

OTHER TITLES IN THE SERIES

THE YELLOW DOG
GEORGES SIMENON

There was an exaggerated humility about her. Her cowed eyes, her way of gliding noiselessly about without bumping into things, of quivering nervously at the slightest word, were the very image of a scullery maid accustomed to hardship. And yet he sensed, beneath that image, glints of pride held firmly in check.

She was anaemic. Her flat chest was not formed to rouse desire. Nevertheless, she was strangely appealing, perhaps because she seemed troubled, despondent, sickly.

In the windswept seaside town of Concarneau, a local wine merchant is shot. In fact, someone is out to kill all the influential men and the entire town is soon sent into a state of panic. For Maigret, the answers lie with the pale, downtrodden waitress Emma, and a strange yellow dog lurking in the shadows...

Translated by Linda Asher

INSPECTOR MAIGRET

OTHER TITLES IN THE SERIES

THE MISTY HARBOUR
GEORGES SIMENON

'A madman? In Maigret's office, he is searched. His suit is new, his underwear is new, his shoes are new. All identifying labels have been removed. No identification papers. No wallet. Five crisp thousand-franc bills have been slipped into one of his pockets.'

A distressed man is found wandering the streets of Paris, with no memory of who he is or how he got there. The answers lead Maigret to a small harbour town, whose quiet citizens conceal a poisonous malice.

Translated by Linda Coverdale

www.penguin.com

INSPECTOR MAIGRET

OTHER TITLES IN THE SERIES

LOCK Nº 1
GEORGES SIMENON

'There was amusement in Ducrau's eyes. In the inspector's too. They stood looking at each other with the same stifled mirth which was full of unspoken thoughts, perhaps of defiance and maybe too of an odd respect.'

A man hauled out of the Charenton canal one night; a girl wandering, confused, in a white nightdress ... these events draw Maigret into the world of the charismatic self-made businessman Ducrau, and the misdeeds of his past.

Translated by David Coward

OTHER TITLES IN THE SERIES

MAIGRET
GEORGES SIMENON

'It was indeed Maigret who was beside him, smoking his pipe, his velvet collar upturned, his hat perched on his head. But it wasn't an enthusiastic Maigret. It wasn't even a Maigret who was sure of himself.'

Maigret's peaceful retirement in the country is interrupted when his nephew comes to him for help after being implicated in a crime he didn't commit. Soon Maigret is back in the heart of Paris, and out of place in a once-familiar world...

Translated by Ros Schwartz

OTHER TITLES IN THE SERIES

CÉCILE IS DEAD
GEORGES SIMENON

'Barely twenty-eight years old. But it would be difficult to look more like an old maid, to move less gracefully, no matter how hard she tried to be pleasing. Those black dresses . . . that ridiculous green hat!'

For six months the dowdy Cécile has been coming to the police station, desperate to convince them that someone has been breaking into her aunt's apartment. No one takes her seriously – until Maigret unearths a story of merciless, deep-rooted greed.

Translated by Anthea Bell

Other Titles in the Series

And more to follow